The Wreck of the Ethie

Aug. 8, 2006

For Tyler Beattie —

The Wreck of the Ethie

Enjoy the adventure —

HILARY HYLAND

Hilary Hyland
& Teddy Bear

PEACHTREE
ATLANTA

ℚ
JR

A Peachtree Jr. Publication

Published by
PEACHTREE PUBLISHERS, LTD.
1700 Chattahoochee Avenue
Atlanta, Georgia 30318-2112

www.peachtree-online.com

Text © 1999 Hilary Hyland
Interior illustrations © 1999 Paul Bachem
Cover illustration © 1999 Linda Crockett

Cover and book design by Loraine M. Balcsik
Composition by Melanie M. McMahon

Photos on pages 106 and 107 courtesy of Maritime History Archives at Memorial University of Newfoundland. Photo on page 109 is from the Gros Morne National Park historical collection. Photos on pages 110, 111, and 112 by Hilary Hyland.

Manufactured in the United States of America

10 9 8 7

Library of Congress Cataloging-in-Publication Data
Hyland, Hilary.
    The wreck of the Ethie / Hilary Hyland; illustrated by Paul Bachem.—1st ed.
      p. cm.
Summary: Fictionalized account of the wreck of the steamship Ethie which occurred on the remote western coast of Newfoundland in December 1919 and in which the dog Skipper proved his heroism.
    ISBN 1-56145-198-3
        1. Ethie (Steamship) Juvenile fiction. [1. Ethie (Steamship) Fiction. 2. Shipwrecks Fiction. 3. Dogs Fiction. 4. Survival Fiction. 5. Newfoundland Fiction.] I. Bachem, Paul, ill.   II. Title
PZ7.H9845Wr 1999
[Fic]—dc 21   99-24706
                                                                                            CIP

For John and Haley
Whose love and support
made everything possible
and in memory of
H. D. "Hoot" Raymond

—*H. H.*

⚓⚓⚓

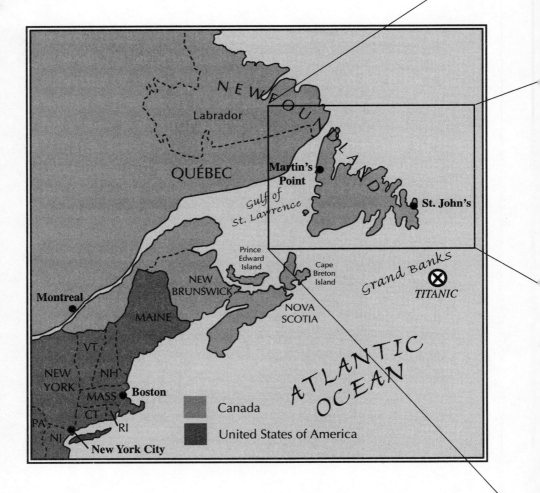

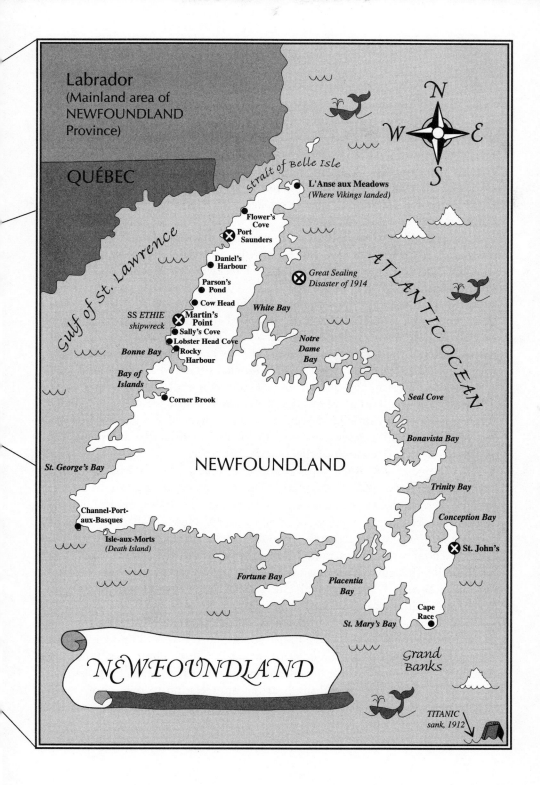

Labrador
(Mainland area of
NEWFOUNDLAND
Province)

QUÉBEC

Strait of Belle Isle

L'Anse aux Meadows
(Where Vikings landed)

Flower's
Cove
Port
Saunders

Gulf of St. Lawrence

Daniel's
Harbour

Parson's
Pond

Cow Head

White Bay

*Great Sealing
Disaster of 1914*

SS *ETHIE*
shipwreck

Martin's
Point

Sally's Cove

Lobster Head Cove

Rocky
Harbour

Bonne Bay

*Notre
Dame
Bay*

*Bay of
Islands*

Corner Brook

ATLANTIC OCEAN

Seal Cove

Bonavista Bay

NEWFOUNDLAND

St. George's Bay

Trinity Bay

Conception Bay

Channel-Port-
aux-Basques

St. John's

Isle-aux-Morts
(Death Island)

Fortune Bay

*Placentia
Bay*

St. Mary's Bay

Cape
Race

*Grand
Banks*

NEWFOUNDLAND

*TITANIC
sank, 1912*

ACKNOWLEDGMENTS

Several friends and supporters helped to make this book a reality. Thank you, Patricia Hunsaker, for being my travel buddy to Newfoundland. It is rare to have a supportive friend who possesses a logical mind as well as an adventurous spirit. Thank you, Jean Enns Rodman, my optimistic friend, for keeping me going and always laughing. I won't forget our agreement. Thank you, Victoria Van Passel McGrath, my talented and artistic friend. It was your idea, to start a writer/illustrator group, and just look now! And for all your help and for all your many kindnesses, thank you, Peggy Jackson and Fred Bowen. What a lucky day when I met you both.

I am grateful to Cheryl Davis, a remarkable marketeer, for her assistance and enthusiasm. And I greatly appreciated the professional publishing suggestions and the common sense advice that I received from my friend Michal Nellans Yanson.

Kathy Hamilton of the Colonial Newfoundland Club and of Old Bay Newfoundlands in Fairfax, Virginia, provided invaluable information about the behavior of Newfoundland dogs at work. Henry F. Picking's suggestions about details of the sea and seamanship and his knowledge of Newfoundland dogs helped me enormously. Judi Adler, co-owner of Sweetbay Newfoundlands in Sherwood, Oregon, also advised me about Newfoundland dogs.

I will be eternally grateful for the professional assistance of Joan Grandy, librarian in the Newfoundland Section of the Provincial Research Library, a part of the Arts and Culture Centre in St. John's, Newfoundland. She was the turning point in my research of this remarkable story.

Also appreciated for their support and assistance are Sherry Mitchell, Kelly Lavin, Judy Slayton, Blanche Forehand, Diane Bramlett Vergouven, as well as Tom Decker, Hilda Menchions, Alyson Raymond, Scott Raymond, and the captain and crew of the *Scademia* out of St. John's, Newfoundland.

For their help in my research, I would like to thank Paula Marshall and Roberta Thomas of the Maritime History Archives at Memorial University of Newfoundland; George Case, Visitor Services Specialist, Gros Morne National Park; Bob Britter, U. S. National Hurricane Center; and David N. Barron, Northern Maritime Research Center in Bedford, Nova Scotia.

A special thanks goes to Paul Bachem for his masterful illustrations.

And for their hard work and enthusiastic support, I wish to thank everyone in the editorial and production departments at Peachtree Publishers, Ltd. I am grateful to Vicky Holifield for her editing expertise and thoughtful suggestions. Finally, I would like to extend my heartfelt appreciation to my editor, Sarah Helyar Smith, for her encouragement, patience, and extraordinary assistance in making this book come to life.

PREFACE

MY DAUGHTER SUGGESTED that I write this book after she read, in a book on Newfoundland dog training, a paragraph describing the shipwreck of the SS *Ethie*. Fascinated with the role of the heroic Newfoundland dog, she couldn't put the story out of her mind, and soon I was captivated too. What began as an entertaining quest to satisfy our curiosity developed into an absorbing project requiring two years of extensive research, numerous interviews, and a trip to that spectacularly wild, enchanting island, Newfoundland.

I based this book on true accounts of the shipwreck of the SS *Ethie* during the Christmas holiday season in 1919. The ship's ninety-two passengers and crew members had the great misfortune to be caught in the blizzard of the century, which pounded the western coast of Newfoundland for several days. I fictionalized some elements of the story, but I tried to remain true to the basic facts of the verified events.

TABLE OF CONTENTS

CHAPTER ONE	MARTIN'S POINT, NEWFOUNDLAND	**1**
CHAPTER TWO	SKIPPER	**7**
CHAPTER THREE	A SEALER'S BOOT	**13**
CHAPTER FOUR	BEFORE THE STORM	**17**
CHAPTER FIVE	PORT SAUNDERS, NEWFOUNDLAND	**23**
CHAPTER SIX	THE ETHIE DEPARTS	**37**
CHAPTER SEVEN	BLIZZARD	**45**
CHAPTER EIGHT	MARTIN'S POINT	**59**
CHAPTER NINE	SKIPPER'S INSTINCT	**71**
CHAPTER TEN	SHIPWRECK	**77**
CHAPTER ELEVEN	SKIPPER BATTLES THE SEA	**83**
CHAPTER TWELVE	RESCUE	**91**
CHAPTER THIRTEEN	ST. JOHN'S, NEWFOUNDLAND	**99**
CARLO—A POEM BY EDWIN J. PRATT		**102**
AUTHOR'S NOTE		**106**
GLOSSARY		**114**

CHAPTER ONE

MARTIN'S POINT, NEWFOUNDLAND

DECEMBER 10, 1919

The huge black dog stood on a cliff overlooking the ocean at Martin's Point. Weighing more than one hundred and fifty pounds, Skipper resembled a bear with a plumed tail. The great Newfoundland was jet black except for a small, white patch on his chest. Wind whistled through his fur, blowing his ears back and flattening them against his head.

The clouds moved quickly across the afternoon sky. Cold air blustered down from the arctic, whirled over Labrador and Quebec, then spilled across the Gulf of St. Lawrence to these rocky bluffs on the northwest coast of Newfoundland. Very few trees or houses stood along the coast to block the wind.

The dog watched the fisherman as he loaded nets into a dory and shoved it into the surf. The tide was still creeping in. Whitecaps dotted the choppy sea just off the Point, and the waves rolling down the Labrador current crashed against the boulders offshore. Known as the Whale's Back, this line of rocks continued for miles along the coast. Visible only during low tide, the treacherous rocks had ruined many ships. Ice was beginning to form along the shoreline, and large chunks floated in the eddies among the boulders.

Skipper knew every cliff, path, and burrow within miles. Opening his mouth slightly and letting his tongue hang out, the dog stretched his head up to the ashen sky. He let the sea spray tingle his throat, and he savored the salty taste. The feathersoft snow melted on his tongue; other flakes landed on his ebony coat, only to be blown away. The polar wind rippled through his fur. The dog faced the ocean and planted his webbed paws firmly on the ground. Watching a flock of seagulls circling above him, he woofed loudly, reminding them that this was his territory.

"Skipperrrrr, me boy. Come on, laddie!" the fisherman called from his boat outside the cove far below. Putting his finger and thumb between his chapped lips, Gerald Reilly whistled loudly. His eyes automatically darted to his fingertips, checking to see if they were turning dark. Several of his fishing friends had lost parts of their fingers in weather like this, so Gerald Reilly was constantly on the lookout for signs of frostbite. He tugged his nippers on over his wool mittens, and silently thanked his wife again for giving him this new pair of thick rubber gloves.

He looked up and saw Skipper cock his head. The dog dashed to the path and picked his way back down the slope to the pebbled beach. The man and his dog had been out several times since daybreak fishing for cod. Mr. Reilly stood in the small fishing dory, his legs wide apart as the boat rocked in the swells. Sea spray dripped off the wide brim of his oilskin hat. When

Skipper reached the water, the fisherman jerked his head sideways, giving the signal.

Skipper knew his job well. He watched as Mr. Reilly lifted the heavy fishing lines and heaved them over the starboard side. The dog stood still while the dark waters sucked the lines under.

It was now high tide and only swirling water marked the rocks that lay not far from shore.

The giant dog breasted a wave washing on the beach and paddled out toward his master. Lifted by a swell, Skipper floated over the Whale's Back rocks and past the white-foamed breakers. Skipper's powerful shoulders and haunches pumped as he cut through the water like a schooner and headed for the fishing boat.

"It's over there, me boy!" Mr. Reilly pointed toward the fishnet. Just beneath the surface of the dark ocean flashed dozens of gleaming lights—the water was teeming with silvery cod.

Skipper swam steadily to the far end of the net, ducked his head under the water, and took the rope in his teeth. Clenching it in his jaws, he circled back to the dory. As he swam, the net closed in on the cod. When Skipper reached the starboard side of the boat, Mr. Reilly grasped the net, secured the rope around a windlass, and cranked the net closer and tighter. Then he hooked each cod and heaved it on board, where it flopped in the growing pile. The fisherman thought about the price he could get for this catch. Once the cod were dried and salted, he could take some of them into town to sell or barter. The rest he and his wife and daughter would store to eat in the long winter months ahead.

Skipper was swimming in circles in the swells. He gazed up at Mr. Reilly and waited for the next command.

Mr. Reilly pulled from under a seat a wooden plank that had strips nailed across it, like steps. He shoved one end into the water and hooked the end he was still holding onto the stern. He gave a short whistle.

Skipper paddled over to the floating plank, scrambled up, and leaped into the dory, scattering fish and flinging water all over Mr. Reilly.

"Whoa there, boy. You got me good!" said the fisherman as he hauled in the plank and stowed it.

Then Mr. Reilly got out the oars and guided the dory around the Whale's Back and into the cove at Martin's Point. As they approached the beach in the cove, the roar of the tons of water crashing against the point gradually dulled.

Skipper stood at the bow, letting the cold wind hit his muzzle. Small icy balls clung to his whiskers and to the tips of his fur. When the boat was ten yards from shore, Skipper sprang into the white froth.

"Here, Skipper," Mr. Reilly yelled as he tossed the bowline toward the beach.

The dog grabbed the rope in his teeth. With strong strokes, the Newfoundland towed the dory, Mr. Reilly, and the load of cod toward the shore.

When Skipper reached the starboard side of the boat,
Mr. Reilly pulled in the net.

Just before the dory beached, Mr. Reilly hopped out, his waders splashing through the water washing back toward the surf. He waited for the next wave to roll up the beach, then commanded, "Pull, Skipper. Pull!"

Holding the rope tight in his jaws, Skipper planted his paws firmly and began to move forward. He timed his pulls with each incoming wave. After a few waves, the dog had managed to haul most of the dory above the waterline.

"Good boy. I'll take it from here," said the fisherman. He looked at the long shadows now stretching most of the way across the cove. "Go on. Off with you till Colleen gets home from school."

CHAPTER TWO

SKIPPER

Skipper's eyes brightened. With his tongue lolling out the side of his mouth, he sped up the rocky path. As he reached the top of the cliff, he knew that he wouldn't see Colleen for a few minutes, so he decided to see what he could find to entertain himself. He put his nose to the ground and picked up a familiar scent. He followed it until he spotted an arctic hare sitting motionless at the edge of the path. Skipper chased the hare into the thicket of scraggly tuckamore trees that grew along the cliff.

With his front half on the ground, his wiggling rump in the air, and his tail twitching, the dog tried to poke his nose through the gnarled branches of the stunted evergreens. He could smell the hare, but he couldn't quite get to it. Flattening his bulky frame against the ground, Skipper felt the cold rocks through the thinner fur on his underbelly.

The needles on the tangled tuckamore limbs pricked his nose. The big dog blinked. Unable to make any progress, Skipper puffed breath out his jowls, snorted, and tried to butt his head through. But that approach didn't work.

The hare refused to be routed. After a couple of minutes of barking and scratching at the ground beneath the branches, Skipper lost interest in the pursuit.

Backing out of the tuckamore, he trotted over to the edge of the cliff. The winds shifted. He sniffed the air, looking south along the shoreline. Every afternoon Skipper waited here for Colleen to come into view as she made her way home from school. He spotted a girl walking along the stony beach. The dog scrambled down the cliff path and dashed across the beach.

⚓ ⚓ ⚓

Colleen Reilly always walked the three miles home from school in Sally's Cove. When the weather wasn't too rough, she liked to take the route along the beach. The beach had little sand, mostly rocks—smooth and rounded to the shape of eggs, worn down from eons of constant scouring by the waves. Some were as large as apples, some small as peas. Many were speckled, pinkish in color, a striking contrast to the gloomy slate-gray cliffs nearby descending into the sea. Accustomed to walking on the rough surface, Colleen kept up a brisk pace, leaning into the icy wind.

A few rays of the late afternoon sun shone through a small break in the heavy, gray clouds. Colleen stopped for a moment, pulled off her stocking cap, and stuffed it in her pocket. Her mittened fingers loosened her tight braids. Her light-brown hair glinted gold in the sunlight. The twelve-year-old girl let the sea air whip her hair behind her before she pulled her hat back on.

The clouds closed up again and shadows crept down the steep slopes that jutted out to the sea. Between the rumbles of the pounding waves against the cliffs around her, she could hear the cry of seagulls. In the distance, far to the south, the muffled baritone of a distant foghorn bellowed its lonely warning.

The girl's eyes watered as the frigid wind blew across her face. Her tongue circled her lips, tasting the briny spray. Shivering, she clutched the scratchy collar of her wool coat and drew it tighter around her neck.

Skipper should be here soon, she thought. Colleen loved scouting among the rocks along the shoreline. All sorts of interesting things washed up. In her room at home she had a box full of shells, bones, feathers, and bottles from her beachcombing expeditions. Sometimes she strapped a canvas sack on Skipper and let him carry the treasures she found. Her greatest pleasure, though, came from finding a small sea animal or bird that needed her attention. A couple of weeks ago she had found an injured puffin and had taken the frightened creature home to nurse back to health.

Colleen heard Skipper's deep, joyful bark. She looked far up the beach and saw him bounding toward her. She waved and cupped her hands around her mouth. "Skipperrrr! Skipperrrr!"

He raced to her with his body low to the beach and his tail straight out behind him. The dog skidded to a stop directly in front of her, his paws plowing into the seaweed. He plopped his bottom down, whisking his tail back and forth. His long pink tongue fell out of the side of his mouth, and his soft eyes searched Colleen's face. Quivering from head to tail, Skipper nudged his muzzle into her outstretched hands and into the warmth of her gloves.

Colleen's eyes sparkled—sometimes blue, sometimes green—like the sea. She bent over and reached around Skipper's neck, burying her face in his shaggy ruff. His undercoat was soft as a fluffy feather pillow.

"Good dog," she murmured. "Good boy."

Skipper cocked his head, listening intently. Colleen cradled his face in her hands, scratching him under his chin. He closed his eyes and lifted his head higher, pressing his chin against her hands. When she gave him a final scratch, he opened his eyes and gave her a slobbery lick right across her freckled nose. Colleen grinned, then wiped her face and stood up.

Skipper nosed among the rocks and pulled out a slimy strand of seaweed. He stood in front of Colleen with the seaweed dangling from his mouth, waiting, his tail wagging eagerly. She grabbed the end and gave it a yank. With a playful growl, the dog pulled on it, jerking his head from side to side.

"I can't hold on, Skipper!" Colleen laughed. "It's too slippery!"

She let go of the seaweed, and Skipper scampered away, shaking his head. The wet seaweed flailed back and forth like a whip. He trotted back and stood in front of Colleen, waiting for her to grab the seaweed again and start another game of tug-of-war.

"C'mon," she said as she headed down the beach. "Let's go get warm."

But soon Skipper, ranging ahead of her, had singled out a stone rolling along the water's edge and proudly carried it back to her. Colleen turned it over in her palm, noticing a black stripe around one end, then threw it just past the breaking waves.

Skipper splashed into the surf and plunged in for the stone. He dove down where the rock had rippled the water and quickly popped back up, a rock softly held in his teeth. He sloshed out of the water, trotted over to Colleen, and dropped it at her feet. A black stripe glistened on one end of the rock. Colleen threw the rock again and again as she walked down the beach, and each time Skipper dove in and brought it back. He never seemed to tire of the game, but after a while Colleen did.

"Come on, Skipper," she called. "It's getting too cold."

The dog ran over to her and shook the water off his long coat, starting with his head and finishing with a last shake at the tip of his tail.

"No, Skipper!" screeched Colleen, trying to get out of the way. "You're getting me all wet!"

She walked on toward Martin's Point, and Skipper loped along ahead of her. He disappeared behind a pile of boulders.

That's when she detected the foul smell. *A dead fish maybe?* Wrinkling her nose, she clambered over the rocks. Skipper was sniffing at a dark object, mostly covered with seaweed, that had washed up on the rocks. Colleen went over and pushed Skipper aside so she could see what he had found. She jabbed at the object with her foot, giving it a shove. It was hard to move. Frowning, she squatted down for a better look. The smell was almost overpowering. Skipper barked and began to paw at the object.

Colleen found a piece of driftwood and pulled the seaweed away. It was a seal hunter's hobnailed boot! The top part of the boot was mangled; it looked as if something had scraped and gouged at it, trying to rip it apart. Colleen shuddered as she thought about the stories her father had told her of sealers lost at sea. Just last year, Alan Raymond, one of her father's friends from Sally's Cove, had gone on a seal-hunting expedition and had never returned. She wondered what had happened to the owner of this boot.

She carefully picked up the boot and looked inside. Holding her breath, she turned the boot upside down. Water spilled out, and something dropped at her feet. She jumped back. It was only a dead crab. She dropped the boot and pulled Skipper away. They hurried across the rocky beach toward home.

CHAPTER THREE

A SEALER'S BOOT

olleen ran down the beach with her long woolen skirt flapping around her legs. Skipper bounded along at her side. They scrambled to the top of a boulder, and the girl scanned the shoreline for her father's boat. The sea mist sprayed her face. She pulled the coat tight again. The sky looked as gray as a humpback whale.

When she caught sight of her father near the dory on the beach, she climbed down off the rock and headed in his direction.

"Papa!" she shouted as soon as she was within calling distance. "Hurry! Come see what washed up this time."

Her father put down the net and walked toward her. "It's a cold day for beachcombing, lassie!" he said, shaking his head but smiling warmly. "What have you turned up now?"

"I'll show you," Colleen said, taking his hand and pulling.

"Well, let's go have a look-see."

As they rounded the bend, Colleen saw that the tide had carried the boot off the rocks. She watched as the water lifted it up and pulled it back toward them. It bobbed up and down in the waves.

"Poor limey. It's a sealer's boot all right. You can tell by the nails on the bottom. Gives 'em traction as they jump from ice pan to ice pan."

"Do you think it came from one of the sealers who was lost at sea last spring?"

"Could be."

"But it's December. Seal season ends in April."

"No matter," said Mr. Reilly, shrugging. "If the owner of that boot did die at sea, his body could have been caught in the currents after the ice melted in the spring. Why, bodies and parts of bodies were washing up a year after the Newfoundland sealing ship disaster five years ago."

"How did that ship sink? Hit an iceberg?"

"Nope. Didn't sink. It was caught in a blizzard. When the storm hit, a party of seal hunters were stranded on an ice field for two nights. By the time they found 'em, more than seventy had frozen to death. Never did find some of the bodies. Many of the survivors lost fingers, toes, or feet from the frostbite. They found a father and son together—their arms frozen solid around each other. It was a sad story all right."

Colleen shivered; goose bumps tingled on her arms. She curled her toes up in her own boots. "Are we just going to let the boot wash out to sea?" she whispered.

Placing his hand gently on her shoulder, he answered, "The unlucky man who wore that boot is buried at sea now. He's in a better place."

The winds were picking up. The fisherman looked at the heavy, gray mackerel sky. "Looks like a change in the weather coming soon, even though the flurries have stopped. Time to head back."

Skipper dashed ahead while Colleen and her father trudged over the stony beach and up the path to the top of the cliff. Skipper reached their cottage first and waited for them by the door. Years of summer sun and the constant battering of the ocean winds had faded their home to a dull gray. Colleen knew from the smoke rising from the stone chimney that it was warm and cozy inside. She and her father had worked last month recaulking the cracks in the cottage with seaweed and mud. She knew how the frigid Newfoundland wind would find the tiniest crack and seep in.

Colleen thought the sturdy, welcoming cottage fit her father somehow. The deep lines on his face reflected his hard life, but his kind smile and the gentleness around his blue eyes drew people to him.

Only two cottages stood on Martin's Point bluff, Colleen's family's and the one down on the point where Mike Lawrence lived alone. Like her father, Mike made his living from the sea.

Colleen wished Mike had children. A girl in particular would be fun—someone to walk to school with, someone to play with and tell secrets to.

The wisps of smoke curling from the chimney beckoned her home. She pulled her hat down over her ears and ran on ahead. Her mother would be inside cooking dinner. Thinking about food made Colleen's stomach tighten; she was hungry.

She stepped up on the small front porch. The floor-boards creaked as she clunked across it in her boots. Colleen could hear her mother's muffled voice through the door. "You'd better get back in that box. Right now! Right now! You hear me?"

Skipper sniffed at the bottom of the door. Whining, he scratched on the door. Colleen paused as she heard a swooshing sound and a crash. She turned the door-knob and carefully pushed the door open. Skipper barreled past her, leaving Colleen standing in the doorway with a view of the dog's plumed tail and her mother holding a broom over her head.

CHAPTER FOUR

BEFORE THE STORM

J ust as Colleen stepped into the room, her mother swatted the broom at a small bird that was waddling quickly around the kitchen, fussing and squawking. White feathers floated in its wake.

Before Colleen could stop him, Skipper joined in the commotion, his tail flying like a distress flag and his hackles bristling. The dog lowered his head and thrust his nose directly behind the zigzagging bird.

"Skipper! No!"

The dog shrank back, head and tail drooping.

With a panicky ruffle of his feathers, the puffin leaped into the rickety crate in the corner. Ever since Colleen had brought the injured puffin home, Skipper had been fascinated with it. He flopped down on the floor with a thud and put his head between his paws. He kept his eyes on the crate, his tail thumping against a chair leg.

Her face flushed, Celeste Reilly placed the broom against the wall. She tucked a loose, yellow-gray strand of hair into the bun at the back of her neck. She folded her arms across her ample belly and shot Colleen and Skipper a stern look.

Cautiously closing the door behind him, Mr. Reilly edged into the room. He hung his coat on the peg by the door.

"Say now, time to eat yet?" he inquired cheerfully.

Throwing her hands up, Colleen's mother scowled and shook her head. But soon Mrs. Reilly couldn't hold back a smile. "Oh, come on in. Supper will be on the table soon," she said, turning to stir a bubbling kettle of cod stew.

Colleen took off her coat and hung it next to her father's. She hoped her mother wouldn't notice the wet footprints on the spotless wood plank floor. Colleen turned to the crate, snug in the corner. Carefully she looked inside, checking the contents. Oblivious to those around her, Colleen cooed softly to the frightened puffin, who was no bigger than a jug of milk. "Don't worry, Puff," she said softly as she examined the bandage around his wing. "I'm here and so's Skipper."

The dog lowered his soft muzzle into the crate only to have the puffin eye him suspiciously. Then the bird pecked at Skipper's nose. Flinching, Skipper drew back and cocked his head, giving the puffin an icy stare.

"Poor thing," said Colleen. "It's scared to death."

"Who's scared?" chuckled her father, peering into the crate. "Puff or Skipper? Don't be a-worryin'. With good doctors like you and Skipper, he'll make it through just fine."

Colleen changed Puff's water as the bird finally relaxed. His eyes fluttered shut and he tucked his head under his wing. "Puff's face looks so funny," she said. "The orange and yellow stripes on his beak and the black lines on his white face make him look like a clown."

"They're brightly colored, they are," her father remarked. "Remind me of pictures I've seen of tropical parrots."

Colleen chuckled. "I can't wait till he's able to fly again. I love to watch them take off and crash-land. Splat! They're so funny looking when they tumble and somersault over the surface of the water." Colleen felt a tad mean laughing at puffins, but their crash landings didn't seem to bother them.

"Puffins look clumsy when they land and take off because of their short, stubby wings and plump bodies," Mr. Reilly said. "But once they get going, they're good fliers, and fast too. Every year they migrate more than a thousand miles to our waters from Iceland. Many of them live on the waters of St. Mary's Bay."

"I declare," snorted Colleen's mother. "It's bad enough that we have a dog that eats as much as the population of St. John's, but now we have this wretched bird to deal with. I've a good mind to cook it for your birthday dinner tomorrow, Gerald. That bird keeps getting out and following me around." She shook her head again as she wiped her hands on her flour-sack apron.

Colleen and her father glanced at each other and tried not to laugh. They knew there was no one more tenderhearted than Celeste Reilly. She liked to act as though she didn't want the animals around, but she was the one who had brought the crate in from the woodshed and lined it with twigs and dried grass. Colleen had even spotted her mother petting the helpless creature when she thought she was alone with it. Colleen couldn't help smiling when she pictured the puffin waddling around behind Mrs. Reilly as she bustled about her chores.

The Reillys sat down at the table and bowed their heads. As her father said grace, Colleen slipped Skipper a piece of bread, which he swallowed in one loud gulp. Peeking through her lowered lashes, she saw her mother extending her hand, sneaking Puff a tidbit. Colleen wished her father would hurry with the blessing. She was starving!

Her thoughts wandered back to the beach and the sealer's boot. She couldn't get the image of the dying seal hunter clutching his son out of her mind.

"Colleen!"

Snapping out of her daydream, she saw her parents staring at her, their eyebrows raised.

"Amen?"

"Amen." Colleen sighed.

Skipper padded over in front of the fireplace and circled twice before lying down. His head rested on his crossed paws, and his tail swished against the rocking chair.

The conversation during dinner floated around Colleen's head.

"Fairly good day today. Maybe it will make up for the light loads last week." Mr. Reilly slurped his stew and wiped the back of his hand across the corner of his mouth. He looked at the clock on the mantel over the fireplace. "I need to finish salting down today's catch."

"Do you think we have enough cod stored now?" her mother asked.

Colleen glanced at her mother. Always a worrier, Mrs. Reilly came from a poor family with six children. Being the oldest, she knew what it meant to work hard and go hungry sometimes. Like most folks on the west coast of Newfoundland, she didn't take winters lightly. When those bitter arctic winds blew, pity the family that didn't have enough wood and food.

"Think so," he answered. "Pulled in more'n fifty cod today." He noticed his wife's concerned expression and added, "I'm sure we have enough. Don't you worry."

After Mr. Reilly returned from doing his chores and Colleen finished her homework, the family went to bed. Colleen slipped her flannel nightgown over her head. The wooden floor felt cold under her bare feet. She quickly stepped onto the hooked rug next to her bed. She blew out the kerosene lamp and leaned over to the windowsill, pulling the bleached canvas curtain to one side. She liked to gaze out the window until she fell asleep.

She couldn't see anything tonight—no moon or stars. *Too many clouds,* she thought. A wind gust rattled the window. She recalled the mare's tail clouds she had seen yesterday and the heavy, ribbed clouds today. Her father's song came to her:

> *Mackerel skies and mares' tails*
> *Make tall ships carry short sails.*

Shivering, Colleen crawled into bed and pulled up the Hudson Bay blanket and the quilt that her mother had made.

Skipper usually slept on the floor next to Colleen's bed. Restless tonight, though, he crept around the room, trying to get comfortable. Turning around several times, he scratched at the rug next to Colleen's bed. He plopped down and rolled over onto his back with his paws crooked over his chest. Eventually he curled up and settled down, and Colleen could hear his long, deep breaths. Soon, he snored. Colleen dangled her arm over the side of her goose feather mattress and let her fingers rest in the warmth of Skipper's fur.

As the family slept, the winds increased, howling around the corners of the cottage and through the tuckamore.

CHAPTER FIVE

PORT SAUNDERS, NEWFOUNDLAND

DECEMBER 10, 1919

The boy awoke from a deep sleep feeling uneasy. He had tossed and turned all night, and the old wool blanket was wadded down around his ankles. Even though he could see his breath in the chill morning air, he was dripping with sweat and his copper-colored hair was matted to his head. Untangling his feet from the tattered blanket, he sat up. Outside, the sky was just beginning to lighten in the east. He could hear the squabbling of the seagulls. The scent of the musty, damp wood and the sharper odor of the briny sea filled his head, making him alert and ready for the day stretching out before him. His blue eyes widened in eager anticipation of his upcoming voyage.

Patrick Logan was a tall boy of sixteen. He easily slid his heavy trunk out from under his bed and twisted the rusty latch. The lid squeaked open. He pulled out his guernsey shirt, boiled wool pants, and sealskin boots. Inside the oilskin bag he found his woolen cap and mitts, knit for him by his mother. He dressed quickly and pulled the cap down almost to his eyebrows.

Born in Belfast, Ireland, Patrick had grown up near the sea. Most of the people in his hometown made their living from the sea or in the local ship-building industry. Other types of jobs were scarce in Belfast. Patrick's father and grandfather had been fishermen. Patrick shared their love of the sea, but he longed for a more exciting life. He had helped his father on the docks from the time he was a small boy, and he had delighted in hearing the sailors' tales of pirates, exotic lands, and adventures on the high seas. Patrick had a burning desire to see more than the docks of Belfast. His dream was one day to become captain of his own ship.

When Patrick was twelve, his uncle had moved to Newfoundland and obtained a coveted berth on the sealing ships out of St. John's. He made good money, so he urged Patrick and his father to come and join him. Patrick was intrigued with the idea of traveling to North America, but a job slaughtering baby seals wasn't what he had in mind. When his uncle offered to help find him a job on a coastal steamer, Patrick began to think seriously about going. One day his uncle wrote him a letter describing the SS *Ethie*, a well-appointed steamer that carried passengers and cargo along the Newfoundland coast. His uncle had served on another ship with the captain of the *Ethie* and respected his knowledge of the sea and his fairness with the crew. Patrick had decided then and there to move to Newfoundland as soon as he was old enough.

Every chance he got, he worked with men from the ships docked at Belfast, little by little learning the skills of a seaman. Soon after his fourteenth birthday, he was able to sign on as ship's boy on a vessel bound for Canada. He sent his uncle a message that he was on his way. His mother had not wanted him to go. She feared that he wouldn't settle down, or worse yet, that he would never return.

When Patrick arrived in Newfoundland, his uncle found him lodgings in Port Saunders and a temporary job as a fisherman's assistant. Patrick knew it would be several months before he would be able to join the crew of the *Ethie*. The cod boat he worked on took him down the coast between Cow Head and the Lobster Cove Head lighthouse. The boat captain's favorite spot was the cove off Martin's Point, near the village of Sally's Cove. Cod and herring were plentiful there.

Patrick enjoyed his work on the fishing boat, but he was glad when the position as ship's boy on the steamer came open at last.

⚓ ⚓ ⚓

Patrick thought his work on the *Ethie* was the perfect job. Always eager to please, he had thrown himself completely into his duties and tried to make himself available to the captain as much as possible. He wanted to prove himself as a sailor. He couldn't imagine life stuck on land. Having been poor in Ireland, he was used to doing without. The crew's simple living quarters on the *Ethie* didn't bother him. Yes, he was in the right place.

As he rushed along the waterfront, he heard someone down by the docks whistling Christmas carols. Patrick loved the cheer of the holiday season, but he missed his mother, father, and six brothers and sisters even more at this time of year. When the *Ethie* reached St. John's harbor in a few days, he would collect forty-nine dollars, his entire wages for this trip.

Patrick had sent his family a small package of gifts months ago, but he still wanted to buy something for his uncle. He looked at a display of pocketknives in the window of Bowrings Store. *When I come back from St. John's,* he thought, *I'll buy him the small one with the ivory handle.* He shifted his duffel bag to his other shoulder and strode briskly down the street, looking forward to joining his shipmates. Weaving in and out among the horse-drawn cabs, he whistled his favorite sea ditty.

The waterfront area in Port Saunders was already crowded and busy. Patrick reached the wharf where the *Ethie* was moored. In the early morning light, the ship's reflection shimmered brown and gray in the water lapping against her wooden hull. Her ropes creaked as they strained and pulled.

Soon she would steam out to sea, loaded with freight, mail, and passengers. Patrick always felt a sense of pride when he saw the *Ethie*. All the crew admired her. No ordinary steamer, she boasted expensive mahogany wood trim, imported Italian tile, stained glass, and skylights—every comfort for her coastal travelers. Ships were the main mode of transportation around Newfoundland, and the *Ethie* had been in constant use since she was built in 1900.

The *Ethie* was bustling with activity. The bo'sun directed the sailors as they loaded large, empty herring barrels into the ship's hold and lashed others above on the deck. The barrels were to be delivered to the St. John's fishermen, who would soon fill them with fish from the Grand Banks, the rich fishing area south and east of Newfoundland.

Captain James Flannery was standing on the forecastle. When he spotted Patrick, he called out, "Aye, boy. Time's a wasting. Better get a move on."

"Aye, aye, sir." Patrick saluted the captain and charged up the gangplank.

Captain Flannery's presence seemed to fill the whole ship. He was knowledgeable and dignified, yet his large callused palms showed that he wasn't afraid to do an honest day's hard work. A severe case of frostbite years back had left a few of his fingers permanently gnarled. The small finger on his left hand was missing, a grim reminder of his brush with death in the great storm of 1914. His curly, sandy-brown hair and close-cropped beard made him look even younger than his thirty-seven years. His steady eyes, however, were the experienced, confident eyes of a seaman who had done and seen much.

Crews respected the captain, and his reputation was one of honesty and fairness. When he gave his word, you could count on it. All seafaring men in Newfoundland knew he had been first mate on the ship that braved the great storm in 1914 to rescue the marooned sealers. The crew admired the captain's courage, and being a superstitious lot, they hoped that his luck would somehow protect them.

Patrick went below searching for Fergus, the chief engineer of the *Ethie*. Fergus was what sailors called a shellback, a veteran seaman. His Irish brogue was thick as a Newfoundland fog. A firm believer in Dr. Chase's kidney liver pills, Fergus swore that they gave him the energy of a mate half his age. Not many would disagree. He was probably too old to be doing the back-breaking work of stoking coal in the ship's furnace, but his loyalty and diligence made him a valued member of the crew.

Patrick was glad to see Fergus, who reminded Patrick of his grandfather, also a wiry old man who loved to tell tall tales. Fergus and the coal stokers who worked for him were having their morning bowls of skillygalee, oatmeal that helped ward off the stomach cramps caused by the smoke and fumes they inhaled.

"Skillygalee, matey?" Fergus said, holding out a bowl.

"No, thanks," Patrick said. "I just came down to see if you could use some help." He looked at the engineer's strong, blue-veined hands.

Patrick often coaxed Fergus to tell his stories of the pirates and corsairs who, years ago, had frequented the waters off Newfoundland. He especially loved the tales of Captain Kidd's buried treasure and hidden gold mine. Fergus always finished his stories of buried gold by quoting Mark Twain: "A gold mine is a hole in the ground with liars standing on top." Then his bellowing horselaugh could be heard from stem to stern.

Fergus had left Ireland as a young boy and moved to the Outer Banks of North Carolina. He had grown up hearing the legends of Blackbeard the pirate and Hatteras Jack, a rare albino dolphin that led ships in and out of the dangerous Hatteras inlet. Fergus even claimed to have seen the ghost of Hatteras Jack with his own eyes. Like most mariners, Fergus considered dolphins a symbol of good fortune.

Today, Fergus was entertaining the stokers with tales of another symbol familiar to all sailors. "St. Elmo's fire," he said, glad to add an eager listener to his audience, "is another matter. It can be either good luck or bad luck, depending on the circumstances," he stated matter-of-factly.

"I was a mate on the good ship *Annabel Grace,* and we were scuddin' off the coast of Ocracoke Island. The day was hot and sultry. I'd just won me hand at whist when the thunder and lightning started. I felt a prickly sensation on me neck. Me hair bristled like the hackles of a dog. The air almost stung, like it had an energy and life all its own. Suddenly, I saw a greenish-blue flame on the masthead of the ship! I looked away in time—for I knew to let the fire's light cover me face was to bring certain death within twenty-four hours. Two or more flames meant that calm weather was ahead for smooth sailin', but one flame meant that stormy weather threatened. We were prepared when the gale hit. After we weathered that storm, we were grateful that St. Elmo's fire had given us warnin' of the approachin' storm."

Patrick could feel his flesh creep. "Have you ever seen it again?" he asked.

Fergus gazed out the porthole and didn't answer for what seemed like a long time. "No. Not likely that I'll get that warning again. But, if you ever see it, take care not to raise your arm up, for that fire will surely jump from the riggin' to your hand, marking you a dead man!"

Before Patrick could ask another question, the old man's demeanor changed. Suddenly he was all business. "We can handle the engine room fine, laddie. Why don't you help the purser with the passenger arrivals?"

Patrick hurried back on deck. He enjoyed helping the purser while he checked the passengers' tickets upon boarding.

Patrick had learned a great deal about other people and places by just watching and listening to the passengers. There would be many exciting places to go when he was captain of his own vessel. Maybe someday he'd sail down to the Outer Banks and get a look at the ghost of Hatteras Jack himself.

Captain Flannery, formal in his blue uniform, stood

on the deck greeting the travelers. The purser punched tickets as the passengers stepped on board, and Patrick helped direct them to their quarters. Patrick watched as the men, women, and children boarded the ship, many carrying gaily wrapped holiday packages. One woman held a baby in her arms. Patrick thought again of his own family and remembered when his little sister was about that age. He wondered what his little sister looked like now.

The twinge of homesickness didn't last long, though. He was too busy guiding the passengers to their cabins. The air was full of commotion. The porters noisily carted trunks aboard. The ship's bell clanged. The seamen in their tar hats sang ditties and ballads to make their work go faster as they loaded the cargo in the forward hold. On the wharf somewhere, Patrick could hear someone playing Christmas carols on the bagpipes.

A sharp voice caught Patrick's attention. "You, there, younker! Assist our servants with these items to our quarters in Cabin A."

"Aye, sir," Patrick responded automatically. He looked up into the stern face of a heavy-set, well-dressed man.

Patrick obediently lifted the bulky travel case from the servant girl's arms and led the man and his party to the ship's most expensive and spacious cabin.

"This cannot be my cabin," the man announced, peering down his bulbous nose at Patrick. "These accommodations are positively pathetic!"

31

Patrick hesitantly replied, "For Newfoundland, sir, the *Ethie* is quite well equipped. I fear that Cabin A is the best we have to offer."

"Oh, indeed. Do not lecture me about any ship in the Reid fleet. This is my first and hopefully last trip from London to this dreadful country. You Newfoundlanders have no idea what truly fine things and living well are all about. It is probably fortunate that you are ignorant of real luxury, as you will obviously never experience the advantages of wealth."

Although Patrick was fuming inside, he ignored the rude comments. He turned to leave, but before he could make his escape, the man blustered, "I say, boy. Go get Captain Flannery. I must have a word with him promptly. Tell him that Reginald Warren has boarded."

"Very well, sir," Patrick responded.

When Patrick returned to the boarding area, the captain was gone. After checking several places on deck, Patrick climbed up to the bridge and looked in the wheelhouse, which was located in front of the smokestack funnels. He found the captain there among the navigational and steering instruments, talking with the first mate.

Patrick waited until the captain finished his discussion. "Excuse me, Captain, a Mr. Reginald Warren would like to speak with you."

"Would he, now?" said Captain Flannery with a sigh and a slight frown. He and the first mate exchanged exasperated looks. "Best to get this over with."

*Captain Flannery, formal in his blue uniform,
stood on the deck greeting the passengers.*

The captain ducked his head under the doorway of the wheelhouse and followed Patrick down to the deck and along the narrow walkway to Cabin A. Tapping his knuckles politely on the cabin door, the captain took a step back and waited until Mr. Warren appeared. The passenger yanked open the door, pushed Patrick aside, and stepped out next to the railing.

"How soon will we be underway?" the passenger demanded.

"We must finish loading the mail, livestock, and other cargo," the captain explained patiently. "We'll be leaving the dock within the hour, on schedule."

"I'm afraid I shall have to speak to the owner of this shipping company," the man said, his voice rising, "if we are late arriving in St. John's." He glanced around, making certain that everyone within earshot could hear how he put the captain in his place.

"I'll do my best, Mr. Warren, but my first responsibility is to ensure that everyone and everything is safely on board before we put out to sea," stated the captain firmly.

The man gave a curt nod and disappeared into his cabin. As they walked away, the captain explained to Patrick, "Mr. Warren is an executive with the Reid Shipping Company, which owns the *Ethie* and the other ships in the Alphabet Fleet."

Patrick nodded. He was familiar with the Alphabet Fleet. He knew that the ships were built in Scotland

and had Scottish names that went down the alphabet: *Argyle, Bruce, Clyde, Dundee, Ethie, Fife, Glencoe, Home,* and so forth.

"No doubt an extremely difficult person to please," added the captain. Patrick didn't respond. He found the man's treatment of the captain rude and embarrassing. On board ship, the captain was always the absolute authority. Patrick supposed that being rich didn't necessarily mean that you had good manners or good sense. That man was as stiff as a schooner's mast. The snob was lucky that Blackbeard wasn't the captain, or he'd be walking the plank by now.

"Come with me, lad," said the captain. They returned to the wheelhouse where the first mate was preparing to pilot the ship out of the harbor and into the Gulf of St. Lawrence. The purser handed Captain Flannery the final manifest. The captain noted that counting passengers and crew, the total number of persons aboard the *Ethie* was now ninety-two.

Captain Flannery made this entry in the ship's log: "8:00 a.m. Wednesday, December 10, 1919; weather conditions good. Sea calm; blue skies prevailing."

⚓ ⚓ ⚓

The SS *Ethie,* on its voyage southward down Newfoundland's west coast, was scheduled to stop at Daniel's Harbour, Parson's Pond, Cow Head, Rocky Harbour at Bonne Bay, and other points to pick up passengers and freight. In three days, they would reach their final destination, St. John's, the capital city on the southeastern corner of the great island.

Patrick remembered the first time he had seen the harbor at St. John's. He had been fascinated by the hills covered with brightly painted houses that looked as if they might tumble right down into the water. He loved watching the fog as it rolled into St. John's, lingering around the colorful houses until their vivid blues and yellows faded into shades of gray. He could almost hear the foghorns bellowing their melancholy warnings as the gloom of dusk settled in on the Narrows, the entrance to St. John's harbor.

So many people and ships. All coming from or going to somewhere far away. One day he would be captain of one of those ships.

Patrick cast his eyes westward over the open sea. It was a cold, glorious day. The skies were a brilliant azure. There wasn't a sign of the mare's tail, cirrus clouds he had noticed around the moon the night before.

CHAPTER SIX

THE ETHIE DEPARTS

The SS *Ethie* steamed out of Port Saunders and headed south toward Bonne Bay, a broad inlet approximately seventy-five miles down the coast.

Patrick went below and helped Fergus in the engine room. When the ship was approaching Daniel's Harbour, Patrick returned to the deck to wait with some of his crew mates until time to unload some cargo and take on more. He had traveled this route on the *Ethie* many times now, but the stark beauty of the coast still took his breath away. He looked forward to seeing the steep cliffs of Bonne Bay again. They reminded him of a picture of a fjord he had seen years ago in a book about an ancient Viking land.

This stretch of coastline was beautiful, but Patrick knew it was also treacherous. He stared in awe at the sheer, vertical cliffs that tumbled down into the sea and at the huge broken boulders and chunks of rock that littered the shore. There were no safe harbors between Port Saunders and Bonne Bay. Sea captains tried to avoid this desolate area when there was any threat of stormy weather. Since the coastline was so dangerous, the *Ethie* anchored offshore at each stop, and smaller skiffs ferried passengers and freight back and forth.

A group of passengers gathered on deck to watch the approach to Daniel's Harbour. Captain Flannery talked with them for a while and then joined Patrick and the other crew members at the rail.

"Aren't those ice partridges, sir?" asked Patrick, pointing to the gulls circling overhead.

The captain frowned, his sandy eyebrows almost coming together over his nose. "They are."

Patrick didn't say anything. He knew the captain was well aware that the pure white gulls from the arctic waters rarely came to shore. When they did, it usually meant that a strong gale was brewing out to sea.

The first mate strode briskly up to the captain and saluted. "The barometer has fallen five millibars, sir," said the mate.

The captain squinted his eyes and scoured the western sky. "I don't like the sound of that," Captain Flannery mumbled to himself. "The air pressure's dropping too quickly. Could be a gale on the way."

Overhearing Captain Flannery's comment about the weather as he passed by, Mr. Warren stopped abruptly and confronted the captain. "Are you mad?" he blustered. "There's hardly a cloud in the sky, and you say you feel a storm coming! I hope this is not an excuse for delaying our progress. I trust that I do not need to stress to you further that we must proceed faster."

"As a matter of fact I considered returning to Port Saunders for a day," said the captain. "When the glass falls more than one millibar an hour, it's never a good sign."

"I've had it with your seaman's tales of superstitions and omens," Mr. Warren said with a dismissing flick of his hand. "The fact remains that it is a clear day, you have a schedule to adhere to, and I am an executive with the company that owns this ship. I insist that we keep to our schedule or Mr. Reid himself will hear of it!"

Patrick noticed that the captain's hands were clenched tightly together behind his back. Captain Flannery was not accustomed to challenges of his authority. He leaned into Mr. Warren's face, so close that his breath made Mr. Warren's neatly trimmed mustache flutter.

"I am in command of this ship, Mr. Warren," he hissed. "Even Mr. Reid will agree to that."

Mr. Warren's eyes widened.

"We will proceed," the captain continued, "not because of your demands, but because this good ship has weathered many Newfoundland gales. And I too will be in contact with Mr. Reid." The captain turned and strode away toward the bridge. He put any thoughts about returning to the safety of Port Saunders's harbor out of his mind.

"Humph," snorted Mr. Warren as he retreated to the sanctuary of his cabin. "We'll see whom Mr. Reid listens to."

⚓ ⚓ ⚓

As the ship slowed, the bo'sun announced their arrival at Daniel's Harbour with three blasts from the ship's whistle. They would exchange more freight and mail here. The bo'sun, who was in charge of the deck crew, ordered the anchor dropped. From the forecastle several seamen released the anchor, and it fell into the water with a clanging roar of the anchor chain.

Patrick paused for a moment and leaned on the rail, listening to the seagulls screeching overhead and the skiffs being lowered into the water. He watched as some small crates were stowed in the skiffs, which the *Ethie*'s sailors then rowed across the water toward the docks. When the loaded skiffs returned, the bo'sun signaled on his silver pipe and the crew began to transfer the passengers and the cargo to the *Ethie*. Patrick helped to load some livestock aboard: an ox, a cow, and a lamb. The lamb bleated pitifully in concert with the squawking gulls. The woolly creature was terrified and fought Patrick with all the strength she could muster. Patrick finally prevailed, and he lowered the lamb gently into the aft cargo hold.

"Don't fret, little one," Patrick said as he patted the lamb's head. "You'll be back on land in a few days." The lantern hanging from the ceiling rocked with the motion of the ship, casting shadows throughout the cargo hold. Steadying the flickering lamp with one hand, Patrick leaned forward and blew out the light.

As the *Ethie* left Daniel's Harbour and steamed down toward Parson's Pond, the cold air became still and heavy. It seemed to hang over the passengers and crew in the darkening haze. At four o'clock, just before sunset, the captain noted in the ship's log that a bank of purple-black clouds was gathering on the western horizon. A blood-red band, often a sign of approaching bad weather, appeared between the clouds and the surface of the ocean. But the sea remained calm. Through the spyglass, the captain watched as the clouds smothered the last waning light. Two hours later as they approached Cow Head, Captain Flannery wrote in the ship's log that the westerly breeze had shifted. It was now coming from the south-southwest. This meant that the *Ethie* was now heading directly into the wind and waves. The sky was black as tar.

While they were anchored at Cow Head, Fergus joined the captain and Patrick in the wheelhouse on the bridge. He gave the captain a quick report on the coal supply, saluted, and turned to go. He stopped next to Patrick and looked out the window at the sky. "There's a gale a-brewin'," the old sailor said under his breath. "I can feel it in me bones. We'll hear the wailing of banshees tonight," he croaked through his tobacco-stained teeth. "They'll be coming. Only the clever or the lucky can escape their grip of death. 'Tis a fact, it is. We need to get away from these cliffs and make it to Bonne Bay soon. We're doomed if a sou'wester hits us along here."

Captain Flannery was studying the barometer. The air pressure continued to drop. He had never seen the barometer drop so fast before, not even during the storm of 1914. The coast below Cow Head was the worst possible place to be caught in a gale. The steep cliffs that rose out of the water formed an impregnable wall. He knew of no coves where they could safely drop anchor and be protected from the wind and waves. Worse, a barrier of rocky shoals guarded the western Newfoundland coast all the way to Bonne Bay.

Fergus' eyes searched the captain's face. He had made many voyages with Captain Flannery, and he had a deep respect for his knowledge of the sea. Still he wondered if he should offer the captain his advice. "We'd best leave the rest of the freight and hightail it to Bonne Bay before it's too late," he whispered to Patrick. "We're as vulnerable as a puffin's belly out here."

But the captain had already made up his mind. "Haul in the skiffs and up-anchor," he ordered the first mate. "We're leaving the rest of the freight. We'll try to make it the forty miles to Bonne Bay before the storm hits."

"Aye, aye, sir."

The bo'sun's pipe sounded, and all hands turned to their tasks. They hoisted up the two skiffs and lashed them into place.

"Batten down the hatches," the bo'sun ordered. Seamen secured portholes, scuttles, and hatchways. The anchor clanked up, and the crew lashed it down.

"Fergus, have the mates stoke more coal," directed the captain. "Get that steam up fast!"

"On my way, sir." Fergus hurried back to the belly of the ship.

It was close to 8:00 p.m. The captain set the *Ethie*'s course at west-southwest. The watch manned his post to keep lookout for the beacon from the lighthouse at Lobster Cove Head, the entrance to Bonne Bay.

At 8:10 p.m. the crew set the taffrail log line, which trailed behind the ship to measure her speed and the distance she traveled. The ship's bell tolled as the *Ethie* rocked in the growing swells. The sea was turning threatening. The waves became more insistent, crashing against the *Ethie*'s starboard bow, and the winds began to shriek up from the Gulf of St. Lawrence. The *Ethie* was still heading straight into the wind. The temperature hovered at freezing.

Patrick tried not to think about the banshees as the cables whipped and snapped in the riggings. The ship's timbers groaned. Patrick wondered if the storm that stranded the sealers in 1914 had begun like this. *This ship has weathered some bad storms,* he reminded himself. *Surely there's nothing to worry about.*

CHAPTER SEVEN

BLIZZARD

Slamming through the waves, the *Ethie* fought her way down the coast. The winds increased and the swells grew higher. As the ship rose and fell, many passengers began to feel queasy and some became seasick. Braving the cold, they crowded onto the deck, hoping the fresh air would provide some relief. At first they stood on the afterdeck, grasping the rail. As the waves became rougher, the motion of the ship sent a few passengers sprawling, coming dangerously close to falling overboard. Holding on to each other, they retreated to their cabins.

Patrick stayed in the wheelhouse, peering into the stormy night. For a short time, the snow let up enough for him to get a good look at the shore. He saw a faint light shining through the windows of a cottage set slightly back from the ledge. Patrick recognized the point of land where the cliff jutted out into the sea. "Look! We're off Martin's Point!" he yelled to the captain. As he spoke, he tasted the cold salt spray blowing in from the southwest. Then without warning, the wind shifted and started blowing from the northwest. The penetrating blasts were pushing the *Ethie* toward the rocky coast. If the *Ethie* hit the barrier rocks, she would be torn to shreds.

Over the howl of the wind, Patrick heard the captain's voice.

"Hard astarboard! Turn her around and head north!" ordered the captain. "If we can't make it back into Port Saunders, we'll try to make it up the Strait of Belle Isle and over to Labrador."

The temperature was falling sharply, and snow began to blow hard in their faces.

"Turn her! Turn her, or we'll crack up on those rocks!" thundered the captain to the first mate. The snow squalls blew thicker, and the waves began to break over the forecastle. As the *Ethie* ground her way through the sea, the scuppers couldn't drain the seawater off fast enough.

Most of the passengers were still huddled in their cabins, clinging to anything that was anchored down. They were scared and confused, having never seen weather change so violently. They watched in terror as water seeped in under the cabin doors. The rocking of the boat tossed their trunks about, and the holiday presents tumbled around on the wet floor.

Lanterns swung wildly. Even pictures that had been bolted to the walls worked themselves loose. The passengers clutched each other, trying not to panic.

The bo'sun sent some extra sailors to work the ship's pumps and others to join Fergus and his coalmen, taking turns shoveling the dusty black lumps into the furnace to keep the steam pressure up. At midnight, the first mate ordered the crew to haul in the taffrail log line because the waves kept pushing it up under the ship. He feared that the line might become entangled in the propeller. The ship was barely making headway.

From the wheelhouse, Captain Flannery watched the waves washing over the upper deck and forecastle. A thin layer of ice shimmered on the rigging, illuminated by the lights on deck. The captain knew that if the *Ethie* iced up with the herring barrels still on deck, she would be so top-heavy from the extra weight of the ice that she would begin to list, and the force of the waves could roll the ship over.

"All hands on deck!" commanded the captain. "Jettison those barrels!"

Freezing spray poured off Patrick's sou'wester. He struggled against the heaving deck and the wind to reach two sailors who were fighting to get one of the bulky wooden barrels overboard. He tucked his head down and pushed his shoulder against the barrel while they strained to heave it over the railing. At last the barrel rolled over the rail and crashed into the water. The rising winds pushed it toward the shoreline boulders. The heavy container shattered on the rocks, and the pieces were sucked under. All that was left was seafoam.

The men labored in the icy wind until they had heaved all the barrels overboard. By three o'clock in the morning, the ship was coated with an inch-thick layer of ice. Patrick rushed down to the livestock in the ship's aft cargo hold. Seawater was seeping in between the creaking planks of the hull. The pumps hissed and clanged, shuddering occasionally with an unnerving scrape. Several drowned rats floated past him in the water. In one corner, he thought he saw the bodies of the ox and the cow. As his eyes adjusted to the darkness, he saw that somehow the lamb had climbed up on a crate and survived. It was struggling to stay on the crate and was near exhaustion. Its matted ribs were rising and falling as it gasped for air. The weak bleats sounded to Patrick like cries for help.

He managed to lift the lamb onto a bigger crate, but he couldn't get the frightened animal out of the hold. He looked wildly around in frustration, realizing that he would need help. Clambering up the stairs, he grasped the hatch and hung on as a wave sprayed over him. He found Fergus in the passageway near the engine room. "Fergus," Patrick called, "can you help me down in the stock hold?"

"Only a minute," Fergus answered, chewing furiously on a plug of tobacco. "Can't leave my mates in the boiler room for long."

The two of them got the lamb to the upper deck, and Patrick tied it to the exhaust pipe behind the wheelhouse smokestack, where it had a little protection.

It was close to 4:00 a.m. The *Ethie*, fighting to stay on her northerly course, was now being driven broadside by the wind and the waves. Patrick had never been so afraid. Tons of icy water poured over the ship and threatened to bury her. She would soon become a floating iceberg in subzero temperatures. Some of the portholes and doors caved in, unleashing torrents of freezing water into the engine room. The main deck was coated with ice. If the *Ethie* capsized, all below would die, imprisoned in an icy tomb.

Long into that bitter cold, never-ending night, Patrick kept a lonely vigil, clinging with one arm to the bellowing exhaust pipe as it belched its soot and smoke and holding the lamb with the other. Through the broken wheelhouse window, he could see the captain at the wheel, trying to regain control of the ship. The snow squalls were so thick that Patrick could barely see the forecastle. His head throbbed. Blood from a cut trickled through a tear in his mitts, but he couldn't feel the pain. His hands were ice numb. He could hear nothing but the screaming wind and the waves pounding against the *Ethie*.

⚓ ⚓ ⚓

In the engine room Fergus and the stokers toiled to keep the boiler going. Bruised and aching from being thrown around in the tossing ship and exhausted from hours of shoveling, they struggled to keep working.

When the coal supply began to run low, some passengers came below and offered their help. They groped around on their hands and knees, gathering up any lumps of coal that had fallen to the floor. Fearing for their safety, Fergus sent them back to their cabins.

Incessant, fierce waves crashed against the *Ethie*'s stern and washed over the deck, cascading through broken portholes and hatches. The seawater hissed as it hit the boiler and turned to steam. Bits of coal on the floor turned into a thick, black muck that stuck to the stokers' boots and hands and coated their faces. Their job became even more difficult when some of the coal in the bin got wet. It would be almost impossible to get the sodden coal to burn and provide enough steam to power the ship.

The choking steam and smoke threatened to suffocate them. Because of the ship's constant pitching, the men fought to stay on their feet to keep from being thrown against or into the fiery boiler. "Don't touch the furnace or you'll get scalded!" barked Fergus. "Take turns holding each other around the waist while you shovel!" The men followed his orders and kept feeding the coal into the jaws of the blazing furnace. The roar of the straining engines almost drowned out the crash of the waves outside.

Several inches of water now covered the boiler room floor. Fergus narrowed his eyes as it sloshed from one side to the other. If the water rose too high, it could pour into the furnace and cause the boiler to explode.

"Sean, you and Thomas start bailin'!" Fergus shouted, handing the men buckets.

*The men followed his order and kept feeding the coal
into the jaws of the blazing furnace.*

The stokers labored on, nearing total exhaustion. They knew that the only hope of survival was to keep the fire going so the captain could keep the *Ethie* away from Newfoundland's cliffs. Their hands were raw and bleeding and their bodies ached, but they kept shoveling.

⚓ ⚓ ⚓

The efforts of Fergus and his boiler room crew kept the *Ethie*'s engines running at full speed. The captain didn't know his ship's exact position, but he figured that if the hurricane-force winds subsided, he would be able to spot the coast of Labrador at daybreak. In the meantime he had to see to the safety of his passengers. The temperature was still falling, and the blizzard seemed to be growing stronger.

Frowning and with deep circles under his eyes, Captain Flannery ordered Patrick and several other crew members to go to the cabins and tell everyone to gather in the salon. "I think it will be the safest place," he said. "Make sure their life jackets are on tightly."

In the swinging lantern light, Patrick noticed that the captain's eyebrows and eyelashes were shuttered in ice. His beard was encrusted with the frozen salt spray, his cheeks blistering red.

Patrick and the other crew members struggled to the cabins and led the petrified passengers along the slick corridors. They held tight to the icy railings, taking care not to slide down or be swept off the ship as it rolled.

Patrick and his crew mates fought their way back and forth from the cabins to the salon, leading each group of passengers. Patrick's frozen mitts were heavy as stones. He tucked his chin into his chest, pushing against the wind with one shoulder as the wind lashed into him. His fingers and toes no longer ached from the stinging cold; they had become numb and leaden.

Reginald Warren was the last to leave his cabin. He refused to budge until his porthole staved in and sea-water began to slosh around on the floor. He joined the other passengers in the salon.

They were clustered together like harp seals on an ice floe, terrified that they were going to perish in the wild sea. There was no panic, only quiet desperation. No hysterical cries, only whimpers and innocent questions from the children who clung to their parents.

Crouched together on the salon deck, shivering under sodden cloaks and blankets, most of the travelers had their legs pulled up under their chins with their forlorn heads resting on their knees. The salon gave them protection from the frigid wind, but their saturated clothes clung to their bodies. The clammy coldness seeped through their hats, mittens, and boots. Some of the adults knew that after the chill would come listlessness and weakness, then finally total numbness. All of the passengers on the *Ethie* knew that their lives depended on the expertise of the captain and his crew and on a break in the weather. Meanwhile, all they could do was look to each other for comfort.

Patrick offered an extra blanket to the woman holding the baby.

"Thank you. I just hope she can continue to sleep," the mother said, wrapping the blanket tightly around her eighteen-month-old girl.

"How she can sleep through this nightmare is beyond me," marveled Patrick.

"She's worn out," said the young mother, who looked exhausted too.

Patrick was concerned about the woman. She was noticeably pregnant and traveling with her elderly grandfather.

"My name is Alice Daren," she said, "and this is little Emily. We are grateful for all your kind help."

"You're most welcome, ma'am," Patrick murmured. He introduced himself and asked what brought them on board the *Ethie*.

She told him she was on the way to St. John's. "I guess I should have delayed our trip," she continued. "We're traveling to St. John's to stay with relatives for the holidays. My husband's working at the Customs Office up in Flower's Cove. He's supposed to join us for Christmas. He'll be so worried with us out in the likes of this storm." What she didn't mention was that she hoped he would be able to see his darling Emily again and their unborn baby, as well.

"I'm hungry, Mommy. My tummy hurts," said a small girl sitting nearby. Her large brown eyes peered out from under a blanket.

"Hush, now," said her mother. "I didn't bring any food with us."

A seaman with icy stubble on his face spoke up. "Ma'am, if it's all right with you, I have a bit of hard tack. Not somethin' she'd want normally, but if she's real hungry...."

"Well, I suppose."

The child's hand darted out. "I'm real hungry," she said.

The seaman dropped the sea biscuit into her tiny out-stretched hand. "She'll have to gnaw on it," he told her mother. "We use hammers to crack 'em up." The old sailor took a swig from a canteen hanging from his belt. "You're welcome to a nip o' my Radway's," he said, holding the container out toward the woman.

The woman shook her head politely.

Patrick smiled. He knew that Radway's Ready Relief consisted mostly of alcohol mixed with hot water or sometimes molasses. The men kept this "medicine" in small canteens that they made from tin cans.

Patrick looked over at Mrs. Daren. Her head was bent and she whispered in prayer. *A miracle is what we need right now,* Patrick thought. He listened to her steady voice and watched her gently stroke her baby's head. He noticed the dark shadows under her hooded eyes. Her wet clothes were frayed, and her shoes were cracked and patched, shabby from constant use. The baby's face glowed peacefully. *How can that be?* he wondered. *There is no peace around here.* Patrick watched the serene rising and falling of the blankets over the baby's chest as she slept. Mrs. Daren began to hum a melody. Other voices joined. Soon all their voices rose together softly and the song seemed to calm their fears for a while.

Patrick was grateful for a moment to sit down and rest. He would soon have to rejoin the other crew members as they struggled to keep the ship away from the rocks. He had almost nodded off when the skylights broke and water poured down on the weary passengers huddling in the salon. Patrick looked out onto the deck. Ice now covered the entire ship, two feet thick in some places! He wondered if the people around him were thinking about the *Titanic,* which had gone down only a few years earlier when she struck an iceberg off the southeastern coast of Newfoundland. His uncle had told him that more than ten thousand ships had perished in the waters surrounding Newfoundland.

All through the wee hours of the morning, the blizzard raged and the winds tore at the *Ethie*. When the sky finally began to lighten in the east, Patrick and some of the passengers peered out, straining to see through the howling storm. All eyes turned to the dark shape looming less than a mile away. They could barely make out the silhouette of some shoreline bluffs.

That can't be Labrador! Patrick thought as he scanned the faint outline of the cliffs. Then a shocking realization sank in. The *Ethie* had made no progress at all! They were still off the coast of Martin's Point, perilously near the ridge of rocks known as the Whale's Back. The pounding surf and winds were forcing them closer to the jagged boulders. Patrick couldn't fight off a feeling of panic.

⚓ ⚓ ⚓

In the wheelhouse Captain Flannery focused his spyglass on the hazardous rocks and then swept it toward the open sea. The blizzard hadn't let up. When he looked to the western horizon, he saw a bank of waves rushing toward them—towers of water as high as the hills of St. John's. Swells piled on swells. As the *Ethie* wallowed in a trough, the wall of water rising next to her looked to be more than seventy-five feet high! A cold dread stabbed his chest.

Captain Flannery had survived blizzards and two hurricanes. But he had never witnessed a storm with such fury as this one.

The *Ethie* nosed up the waves and plunged back down as the tip of each wave broke over the ship. The captain was afraid the ship would pitchpole—flip end over end from the force of a breaking wave. The waves continued to gain power and hurl themselves against the shore. The sea boiled foam. Reeling from exhaustion, the bleary-eyed captain began an entry in the ship's log: Daybreak, December 11, 1919. He let the pen slip from his half-frozen fingers, and his shoulders sagged with disbelief and despair.

CHAPTER EIGHT

MARTIN'S POINT

Colleen awakened to the smells of buttermilk biscuits baking and coffee brewing. She heard her parents in the kitchen, but she wanted to sleep longer. The screaming winds had waked her several times during the night, and she hadn't gotten much sleep. She opened her eyes a crack and looked at the pale light coming through her window. Then she remembered. It was her father's birthday. *I should get up,* she thought. *But the room's so cold, and I'm so sleepy. Maybe I can stay in bed a little longer.* She turned over and closed her eyes again.

Skipper's tail began to thump against the floor. Colleen lay still, hoping he would think she was still asleep. No such luck. Skipper poked his wet nose under the covers and nudged her elbow. "Aaaaaagh. Leave me alone, Skipper!" she cried. "You rascal!"

Skipper playfully jabbed Colleen with his cold muzzle until she surrendered. She stretched and rubbed her eyes. The wind screeched around the house, rattling the windows and doors. Cold air seeped under the crack below her window. She jumped out of bed and dressed quickly, eager for something warm to drink.

As she walked into the kitchen, Colleen greeted her father with a cheerful "Happy birthday." He didn't answer. When she saw her parents' faces, she knew something was wrong. *Is the storm that bad?* she wondered. She ran to the window and looked out. The wind whipped the snow against the glass panes. Mounds of snow had drifted against their cottage. They were in the middle of a blizzard! Colleen looked back at her mother and father. She could see the strain on her mother's face. The last time a storm like this had hit Martin's Point, her family had been snowed in for several days.

Her father's birthday forgotten, Colleen ate her oatmeal and drank her tea in silence and then helped her mother clear the table. Mr. Reilly stood by the window, watching the blowing snow and scanning the skies for a break in the storm. Skipper stationed himself near the door. Colleen tidied up Puff's crate and refilled the puffin's water dish, then went back to her room. She pulled a book out of the shelf and settled down to read. It was going to be a long morning.

⚓ ⚓ ⚓

Between the roar of the wind gusts, Patrick could hear the whine of the engines below. He knew Fergus and the stokers were doing their best to keep the steam pressure up and the *Ethie* away from the rocky coast. It was now midmorning, and the storm hadn't let up; the winds were still driving the snow so hard that the flakes stung Patrick's cheeks. Between rifts in the walls of white, Patrick studied the grim shoreline, trying to estimate how far they were from Martin's Point. *The winds are too strong,* he worried. *We'll never be able to get back out to sea.* Patrick knew the area well because he had often fished this stretch of coastline when he was working on the fishing boat. *If the wind keeps up at this force,* he thought, *we'll be blown onto the rocks. If only we could make it into the cove beyond the Whale's Back.* Patrick hesitated to go to the wheelhouse to offer his help. The captain and the first mate were surely far too busy to talk to him. *But maybe my knowledge of the shoreline would be of some help to them.* Patrick made up his mind to give it a try.

Since the salon doors were frozen shut, some sailors hoisted Patrick through the broken skylight. He carefully made his way to the bridge. Captain Flannery was coming out of the wheelhouse with Fergus and the first mate. The howling wind, the crash of the waves, and the roaring engines made it hard for Patrick to make himself heard. He shouted louder to the captain, jabbing his finger toward the cliff. "Sir, look yonder! We're still off Martin's Point. I know this area well. I've fished here many times." He paused to catch his breath, gasping as the frigid air pushed down his throat.

"Yes, lad! We've studied the map," the captain yelled over the noise of the storm. "Do you know of any place along here where we could beach the ship?"

"Yes sir, there's a cove we can try to steer her to," Patrick said. "Martin's Point bluff extends out into the shoal waters. The Whale's Back protects the cove's channel. The rocks are below water except at low tide. But since the sea is so high from this storm, with a bit of luck we might be able to maneuver the ship over the shoals and run her aground in the cove just south of the point. 'Tis a long shot to be sure, but we might have a chance that way."

The captain considered Patrick's suggestion. The winds were forcing them toward certain destruction. If the *Ethie* struck those shoal rocks before they made it to the cove, the ship would be torn apart, and they would all drown. The water was creeping higher in the engine room, increasing the likelihood of an explosion. The captain looked at Fergus, the first mate, and the bo'sun, then toward the salon where all the passengers were huddled together. Finally he nodded. They had to try to get the ship into the cove. "We'll try it, men," said the captain. "All hands back to your posts." He turned to Patrick. "Come with me to tell the passengers."

Patrick and the captain slipped and slid along the passageway, gripping the rail to keep from being thrown overboard. They made their way to the area above the salon and lowered themselves down through the broken skylight.

The captain addressed the frightened passengers. "We're in a dire predicament," he said, "and we have run out of options. We've decided to beach the *Ethie*."

The exhausted passengers gasped.

"Check your life jackets. We'll pull the women and children up through the broken skylight to the deck. Their chances of survival will be better there. Patrick, help the other seamen get them on deck, then come to the wheelhouse. Since you know the shoals, you'll be my navigator."

One of the passengers pushed forward. "This is preposterous!" shouted Mr. Warren. "You cannot be serious, intentionally running this ship aground! We'll all be killed! Mr. Reid didn't place you in charge of this ship to wreck it!" The man's eyes bulged as he screamed at Captain Flannery.

The captain coolly stared into Mr. Warren's eyes. "We have no other choice. Mr. Reid would do the same thing if he were here."

"He's not here and—"

Cutting him off, the captain replied, "That's right, he's not here and I'm in charge. Now get out of my way. We've work to do!" He climbed out through the skylight and returned to the wheelhouse.

In spite of Mr. Warren's outburst, no one panicked. Calmly the crew instructed the passengers about what to do. Fathers hugged their wives and children. Patrick and the seamen hoisted the women and children up to the deck where they huddled together, holding on for dear life atop the pitching, iced-over ship. Wee Emily Daren began to cry as the wind whipped open her blanket, exposing her to the stinging snow and spray. The swirling wind snatched her wail and threw it away from the ship. Alice Daren wrapped the blanket tighter and tried to shield her baby with her body.

In the wheelhouse, Patrick watched the captain with admiration. Captain Flannery was surely thinking of his own family and how much he loved them, wondering if he'd have another Christmas with them. Yet he stood at the wheel steadily, alternately glaring at the cliffs then out to sea. This Newfoundlander had seen the sea win before, but he was determined to fight on.

Patrick looked back at the cliffs and scanned them closely. "There it is, sir, the cove," he said, pointing to the break in the cliffs.

Captain Flannery nodded. "Put the wheel hard astarboard!" the captain ordered the first mate. The captain straightened his shoulders and braced himself as the sleet and frosty wind blew through the broken windows and pelted his face. He didn't flinch, even though he knew he had just ordered the *Ethie* to make her final run.

Suddenly a slip hook gave way, and the wind tore one of the lifeboats from its davits. It careened along the deck, breaking the rails. It shattered one of the frozen portholes to the engine room, sending a torrent of icy water over the fatigued crew below.

Still battling in the coal's mire on the sticky floor, Fergus and the exhausted stokers stiffly shoveled more coal into the furnace. The captain needed plenty of steam pressure to keep the *Ethie* under control so he could drive her ashore.

Fergus yelled to his men, "If any of you want to go up top, I won't hold it against you. It's every man for himself. But if we fight together, we've a chance to make it."

Some of the men sloshed around nervously in the mucky water as the engine's pistons clanked and hissed. But no one left. One of the firemen grinned shakily and exclaimed, "Fergus, we all started this voyage together and we'll end it together! One way or another."

Fergus choked up from more than the smoke in the engine room. These were poor, hardworking men, many born in Ireland, England, or Scotland. Dreamers all, they had moved from their native countries to have a chance for a better life. But there in that watery inferno with little hope of escape, these men stubbornly resolved to fight on together against the wrath of the storm. They were determined not to let each other down.

Fergus nodded and jammed his shovel into the coal bin and raised his fist. He shouted, "On my mother's eyes I swear: we are Newfoundlanders all, and we won't go without a fight!"

An encouraging cry rose from the men as they bent to their shovels once again. They heaved the coal feverishly, harder and harder, until new rivers of perspiration streamed down their blackened faces. The engine room was stifling hot. Scorching steam choked them. They hacked and coughed as the suffocating heat from the boilers almost strangled them. But the pressure slowly began to rise.

The seamen on the bridge watched the shoreline nervously. "Permission to announce our arrival, Captain," requested the bo'sun. Under normal circumstances the bo'sun gave the ship's whistle three sharp blasts as they approached a harbor to moor.

Patrick looked at the captain. They wouldn't be docking the *Ethie* this time, but beaching her. This would be her last trip.

With a grim smile tugging at the corners of his mouth, the captain tilted his head and nodded his approval. "Announce us loud and clear, bo'sun," he ordered. "Maybe someone ashore will be able to help once we're aground." He stepped up to the wheel.

So their course was set. The bo'sun tied down the ship's whistle and let it blast. The battle between the ship and the unrelenting gale had lasted nearly sixteen hours. It was noon on December 11, 1919. The *Ethie* had survived the hurricane force winds so far. *How much longer can she continue to fight?* Patrick worried. *How much more can a wooden steamer take?*

With the ship's whistle screaming and the propellers churning at full speed, the passengers and crew braced for the shipwreck. The *Ethie* was now pointed toward the Whale's Back rocks and the cliffs of Martin's Point. Patrick, his hands gripping the windowsill, stood next to the captain in the wheelhouse, peering ahead at the shoreline through the broken windows. He turned his gaze toward the sea behind them, holding his hand up to protect his eyes from the onslaught of the wind and snow. A sickening feeling rose in Patrick's stomach as he saw a monstrous wave coming at them. It looked higher than the cliffs that towered before them! Strengthening and looming even higher, the wave bore down on the struggling ship.

The passengers could only watch, terrified, as the wave sucked the water back from the peaks of the Whale's Back rocks. The ridges were visible almost to the sea floor. The wave hesitated, rolled under the *Ethie*, and crashed down on the boulders, then surged onward to Martin's Point.

But the *Ethie*, her stern pointed up and her bow down, was caught in the force of the next wave as it broke over her. The ship plunged down the backside of the wave—more than fifty feet in the white froth. A terrible screech and jarring from astern shook the ship.

"I've lost the steering, sir!" the first mate shouted. "The stern post and rudder must've been ripped off!"

The *Ethie* was careening out of control! But just before the rushing waters could hurl her onto the rocks, a third wave caught the ship and lifted her back up.

Patrick held his breath. Fergus had once told him that all monstrous waves come in threes. "These big waves pound the coast three times," he had said, "and then you have a moment of eerie quiet. Then the terrible onslaught begins again."

Patrick was nearly paralyzed with fear. The ship's chronometer in the wheelhouse showed that it was 12:30, but the midday sky was so gray that Patrick thought it could have been almost evening. Looking back over the ship's stern, Patrick hollered, "Look! There!"

The captain was concentrating on the rocks before him. When he heard Patrick's cry, he jerked his head around. Another avalanche of water was bearing down on them. The wall of water grew higher and higher. Blown by the swirling gusts, the *Ethie* swung around to face her enemy head-on. Everyone on board saw the wave surging toward them. Not a single person thought they would survive.

But this wave didn't break over the ship like the last one. Instead, the enormous wave lifted the *Ethie* up and swept her over the Whale's Back ridges and dropped her inside the waters of the cove. For a moment the passengers and crew dared to hope they might have a chance. They cheered, but the sight of the cliffs now looming high above them made them gasp and try to brace themselves.

Within a few hundred feet of the cliffs at Martin's Point, the *Ethie* slammed broadside into the shore reefs.

Patrick was hurled against the wall of the wheelhouse. He called to the captain and the first mate and felt a rush of relief when he heard their voices reply. The three of them crawled to the door and made their way out onto the icy bridge. Patrick was horrified at the scene before them. The impact of the collision had rammed the steel plates on the ship's underside up through the deck. The *Ethie* was teetering on the rocks like a piece of bait over a hungry shark's mouth. And the sea was closing in.

CHAPTER NINE

SKIPPER'S INSTINCT

A little before noon, Colleen went back into the kitchen.

"The storm doesn't seem to be letting up," her father said. "I'm going out before the snow gets too deep." Mr. Reilly put on his heavy coat and boots.

Skipper stood up and stretched, his tail thumping hard against the door.

"Be careful, Gerald," warned Colleen's mother, wrapping a scarf around his neck.

"It's a bad one out there all right," he said. "We've probably got enough firewood stacked next to the house, but just in case I'll fetch some more from the big woodpile. Expect we'll be homebound for a few days from the looks of this storm."

Skipper watched as Mr. Reilly pulled on his oilskin mitts, then yanked his cap down firmly over his ears. When the man took the harness off the hook, Skipper trotted eagerly over to him and stood patiently. Mr. Reilly slipped the harness on him. The big Newfoundland often pulled loads of firewood across the snowbanks. Skipper looked up at him, his eyes bright.

Thrusting her chin out, Colleen announced, "I'm going, too."

Her father opened his mouth to say no, but he could see she had made up her mind. Glad to have her help, he nodded and said, "Come on, then. But you'd best bundle up real well."

Colleen grabbed her hat and coat, put on an extra pair of wool socks, and stepped into her boots. Mr. Reilly opened the door a crack and the wind blew it against his shoulder. He held the door while Skipper edged out and scrambled over the snow piled up on the threshold. Colleen and her father pushed out together and slowly made their way along the trail that Skipper had plowed through the snow, which was well above Colleen's knees. They struggled through the storm to the hut where the sled was stored. They had to lean on each other to keep from falling.

The fierce winds swirled over the snowdrifts, whistling around the tuckamore and down the cliffs. Mr. Reilly shook his head. "Haven't ever seen a blizzard like this one." He called Skipper and attached the ropes on the sled to the harness.

"Let's go, boy!" he shouted.

Skipper didn't hesitate. As he plowed ahead, his chest strained against the harness straps. He lowered his head, protecting his eyes from the blinding assault of the snow. Mr. Reilly and Colleen followed in the new path that Skipper created in the snow to the pile of logs near the edge of the tuckamore. Even though the temperature was well below freezing, Skipper panted, steam blowing from his mouth and nose. The hard-driven snow peppered his tongue. It seemed to take forever to go a short distance, but they finally reached the woodpile. Mr. Reilly knocked ice off the logs and loaded them onto the sled. Colleen's hands were so cold that she could barely grasp more than one log at a time.

They were halfway back to the house when Skipper paused and lifted his huge head into the wind, looking toward the sea. His nostrils flared. He sniffed, then snorted. He cocked his ears and stood still, his body tense. Suddenly the dog twisted, jerking on the traces of the harness. Barking furiously, Skipper thrashed around, trying to wriggle out of the harness.

"Unhitch the harness, Papa!" Colleen yelled. "Skipper's heard something!" Then she paused and looked toward the ocean. "What is that noise?"

Mr. Reilly unfastened the harness and the dog took off, bounding through the snow toward the cliff overlooking the cove.

"Skipper!" Colleen and her father called. The dog halted, glanced back over his shoulder, and then ran on. Skipper wasn't playing. Curious at first, then worried, Colleen and Mr. Reilly followed him.

When they reached the top of the cliff, the snow lessened. Then Colleen saw it. A hundred yards from the rocky beach a ship was wedged broadside in the cove. She couldn't believe her eyes. A shipwreck? Through the swirling snow, she thought she could make out the dim forms of people on deck. Towering waves rammed

The thundering surf, jagged rocks, and enormous waves made it impossible to get ashore.

the ship. Between gusts of wind she could hear clearly the mournful wail of the steam whistle.

Colleen gasped, feeling the bitter cold in her lungs. She put her hands up to shield her eyes from the blowing snow and squinted at the scene below. A receding wave had pulled the ocean waters away, revealing boulders deep on the ocean's floor. The ship teetered toward the rocks, looking as if it might lurch onto them at any moment. Beyond the ship she saw a bank of waves that looked like moving mountains. They grew higher and higher until they seemed to touch the clouds.

When she thought they couldn't possibly get any taller, the waves smashed onto the rocky shoals. Tons of water crashed down on the battered ship. The ocean exploded forward, hitting the cliffs. The waves clawed for the top, and then the churning waters receded into the black fury of the sea. The cove was being completely engulfed by the surging waves.

Her father looked on, stunned. "That ship is doomed," he said, shaking his head.

"All those people will die unless we can help them!" exclaimed Colleen. "What can we do?"

"Hurry back and tell your mother about the wreck. Gather up as many blankets, ropes, and chains as you can find!" shouted her father, who turned and began to wade through the snow along the cliff.

"But where are you going?" Colleen asked.

"I'll get Mike Lawrence and the dory. We'll meet you down there," he replied, pointing down to the cove.

Skipper barked several times at the ship, bounding back and forth at the top of the path that led down to the beach.

Colleen scrambled back toward the cottage, struggling to keep the wind from knocking her into the deep snow. "Come on, boy!" she called to Skipper.

The dog hesitated, looked at her, then back at the ship. Again he barked toward the ship, then ran back and forth at the cliff's edge like a trapped wild animal. His eyes rarely left the ship. Colleen yelled once more, "Come on! Skipper!" *That dog is acting so strange,* she thought. *He hardly ever ignores my commands.* She hurried on toward the cottage without him.

CHAPTER 10

SHIPWRECK

In the steam-choked engine room, Fergus and his men groped around, trying to assess the damage. Icy ocean water poured in through the puncture hole in the hull.

"Shut down the furnace!" yelled Fergus. "She's staved in!"

As the seawater rose in the engine room, his men hurried to shut down the furnace, knowing that the boiler could explode at any second.

As soon as the job was done, Fergus ordered, "Open the door! Everyone out!"

"It won't open!" shouted a fireman. Several men grappled with the ice-locked door. It wouldn't budge. They were trapped and the water was rising.

"Try the ventilator shaft!" barked Fergus, black smoke filling his throat and lungs. One by one, the men scrambled out through the shaft. When they reached the deck, gasping for air, they looked around in horror at the wrecked ship. They were relieved to see that the other crew members and the passengers, although shaken, appeared to be uninjured. Fergus climbed to the bridge and stood next to Patrick.

Patrick looked toward the shore. They were only about a hundred yards away. But they might as well have been a hundred miles away. The thundering surf, jagged rocks, and enormous waves made it impossible to get ashore.

As the wind, snow, and relentless waves hammered the *Ethie*, she lurched, creaking and moaning. When she tilted abruptly, passengers and crew slid across the iced deck, scrambling and grabbing at anything to hold on to. Patrick knew the *Ethie* couldn't withstand the sea's battering much longer. When she broke up, they would all surely drown.

The ship shook again; timbers splintered. The smokestack funnel cracked, belching smoke and soot.

Patrick watched helplessly as the lamb was swept across the sloping bulwarks and over the side. "Avast! Nooooo!" Patrick's and the lamb's eyes connected fleetingly before the animal disappeared into the sea. A bitter taste rose in Patrick's mouth. His head felt like it had been smashed with a sledgehammer. Sick at heart, he leaned against the side of the ship and threw up. Tears began running down his face, freezing before they dropped from his chin. He didn't bother to wipe them away. He rested his head on his folded arms. *All is lost,* he thought. *I don't want to die.*

Then out of the corner of his eye Patrick thought he glimpsed a movement on the shore. He lifted his head and strained to see through the stinging snow and wind. Some people were jumping around on the rocky beach, waving their arms. Patrick yelled and pointed, "Look! Look! They see us!" He kept shouting until the captain and all the passengers spotted them, too.

Captain Flannery took charge immediately. "Attach a lifeline to that ring buoy and we'll try to float it to shore. Then the people on the beach can secure the line so we can rig up a breeches buoy or a bo'sun's chair to carry people from the ship across to safety."

"It's a long shot," Fergus said to Patrick, "but what else can we do?"

As the captain shouted orders, the crew fastened the rope onto the buoy. They shoved it over the side of the ship, watching as the line snaked down into the blackness of the sea. The buoy bobbed back up and floated the rope in toward the shore, but the line became snarled on the rocks. The seamen managed to haul the buoy back and relaunch it several times, but each time their efforts failed. On the last try, the rope snagged between the rocks, and the crew could not pull it loose.

"Let's launch the mail boat!" Fergus suggested over the noise of the wind. "We could cut the rope loose and carry the line to shore."

"That skiff could never endure the surf or those rocks," worried the first mate.

"Well, let's give it a try. We've nothing to lose at this point," declared Captain Flannery, wiping ice from his brow with his frozen mitts.

Turning to the crew assembled near him, the captain thought a moment, then stated, "I cannot in good conscience order any man to undertake such a dangerous and foolhardy mission. But if some of you wish to try, I won't stand in your way. Two must attempt it together, though, because one person could never manage the oars."

The crew muttered to one another, discussing the risks of taking the mail boat through the stormy waters past the rocks. Dejected, the passengers just looked on. Mrs. Daren shrugged, sadly shaking her head. "It would be a quick death, to be sure," she said.

Patrick spoke up. "I'll go!"

"No!" boomed the captain. He couldn't mask his fondness for the boy.

"Please, sir. I know this cove. I'll have a chance if someone will go with me. We must at least try. We can't give up now after fighting so hard. Not after all we've been through!"

Fergus stepped forward and said, "'Twas my idea. I'll go too."

Patrick was shocked. Was he actually serious? He was too old.

"As the lad said," Fergus added, "if we don't try, we'll all perish."

The captain sighed, then consented. "Very well," he said. "I'm proud of you both." It was settled.

One seaman used a sledgehammer to knock the ice off the davits of the mail boat while others quickly knocked ice off the upturned hull. They swung the skiff over the rail. Fergus climbed in and held his hand out to Patrick. The young man pushed away his fear and stepped into the boat. Another seaman handed Patrick a sturdy knife to cut the snagged rope. Then the crewmen lowered the small craft into the ocean. Even in the lee of the *Ethie*, the sea lashed at the boat and smashed it against the side of the ship. Within seconds, the mail boat split open and began to sink.

Patrick reached for the bowline, which was still attached to the *Ethie,* and held on. Fergus clung to his leg. Patrick grappled with him and finally lifted him up so he could grasp the line. Slowly, they managed to pull themselves back to the ship where strong hands hauled them back on board.

Patrick lay on his back on the icy deck, choking and sputtering. His lungs ached as he inhaled the frigid air. The captain and several sailors helped the two men to their feet. Patrick shivered violently as his soaked clothes sagged around his body. He leaned against the captain to keep from keeling over. Glancing back toward the shore, he gasped. In a hoarse voice he croaked, "Look!"

An awed murmur echoed among the passengers as they stared toward the beach.

CHAPTER ELEVEN

SKIPPER BATTLES THE SEA

olleen and Mrs. Reilly hurried down the path to the beach, carrying blankets and ropes. The intense cold had already numbed Colleen's fingers and toes until they no longer hurt. Her legs felt as heavy and as stiff as the dory's anchor. Her wool cap was covered with ice, and her long hair whipped around her face in the wind.

By the time she and her mother reached the beach, Mr. Reilly and Mike Lawrence had hauled the dory to the water's edge. Colleen looked at her father. His eyebrows were caked with ice and his face was blotchy red. His lips set in a grim line, Mr. Reilly gripped Skipper's harness with both hands. The Newfoundland strained against the harness, never taking his eyes off the foundering ship. Desperate, the two men tried to think what to do. It was an impossible situation. The storm continued to rage.

Colleen and the others watched as some people from the ship tied a rope to a buoy and attempted to float it ashore. They tried again and again, but each time the line caught on the rocks only a few feet from the ship. Mike Lawrence and Mr. Reilly waited, hoping that the winds would let up enough for them to make a run out to the ship with their dory.

"Look!" cried Colleen. "They're trying to put in a boat!" The four of them looked on in horror as the churning water slammed the boat against the ship, splintering the skiff like matchsticks.

"It's hopeless," said Mike Lawrence, turning away sadly. "Our little dory could never make it in this storm."

Colleen's father and mother didn't say anything.

"We can't give up," Colleen moaned. "There must be a way!"

"There's nothing we can do!" shouted her father. "If we could get the rope, we could rig it up to that tree at the top of the cliff. But it's impossible to get near the ship. Look at the ocean! I've never seen the likes of a storm such as this. Never!"

"But Papa, what about Skipper? Couldn't he swim out to the ship and bring the rope back to us? He's pulled your heavy fishing nets hundreds of times. He can make it. I know he can!"

"No, Colleen. He'll be killed. No living being can make it through that dreadful surf. Not even Skipper. We'll have to wait till the sea calms down."

"We must try, Papa. Please! They'll all be killed if we don't do something now. We can't just stand here and watch them die. I know Skipper can save them!"

Colleen glanced at her mother, who avoided her daughter's eyes. Mrs. Reilly sadly shook her head and tried to blink back the tears. She closed her eyes and made the sign of the cross across her chest.

Colleen ran over to Skipper, who stood staring at the ship, and knelt down beside him.

Mr. Reilly watched his daughter and her beloved dog. Colleen looked up at her father and pleaded with her eyes.

Cursing fate under his breath, her father agonized at their helplessness. This tragedy now might reach out to touch the person he loved the most in the world, his daughter. If Skipper drowned before their eyes, Colleen would be haunted forever by the memory.

He was desperate. They either had to convince themselves that the ship's destiny was out of their hands and do nothing, or they had to act. Either way, they would have to live with the consequences. Mr. Reilly could see that sending Skipper was the last glimmer of hope for the people on that doomed ship. But Skipper was Colleen's dog. It would be her choice.

The Newfoundland leaned into the harness, eager to be released. His eyes, usually soft, were as hard as steel. He barely felt Colleen's arms around his neck, her head buried in his fur.

She lifted his large head in her hands and stared into his eyes. "It's up to you, Skipper," she said. "I know you can do it!"

Her heart stirring, Colleen slipped the harness off the dog and stood up. She stretched out her arm, pointing to the ship. "Go, Skipper!" she cried. "Go get the rope! Go!"

Skipper dashed straight into the pounding surf.

The thundering wind paused, collected itself, and intensified. The deafening roar whipped the waves to new heights.

As soon as Skipper hit the cold water, a wave curled up before him, hovered, and then closed over him. He swam steadily through the foam until another wave lifted him up. Battling through wave after wave, his tail steadied him like a rudder as he neared the shoals.

Colleen held her breath, hoping. She caught a glimpse of his bobbing head. A wall of water swelled up, heading directly for the dog. "Skipper!" Colleen shrieked.

Skipper kept paddling. This time, instead of lifting him up, the wave broke above him and sent tons of water crushing down on him. The wave flipped the dog over backward and forced him down against the rocks. Water filled his nose and throat. The undertow pulled him deeper under the water. His lungs ached and he couldn't catch his breath. He was choking.

But Skipper fought against the raging seawater. He stretched upward, reaching harder with his forelegs, climbing invisible, watery steps. The dog's eyes burned. He struggled out of the darkness toward the murky light. The furious waves above him were now only a loud rumble. Finally he exploded through the ocean's surface. Coughing out the salty water, he inhaled great gulps of cold air. Shuddering, Skipper turned his blood-shot eyes toward the ship and kept them fixed on it.

Only his head was above the water. He kicked and paddled through the currents, struggling to keep his nose above water. His nostrils flared, seeking more air. His ears were flattened against his head, but water still trickled in. The crashing waves and screaming wind blended to a dull roar. Shaking his head, he tried to clear his ears.

The undertow had drawn Skipper closer to the ship. He could see the faces of the people on the deck, their arms waving frantically. They were calling to him, pleading with him not to give up. He heard a baby wailing.

Skipper swam on. Blood streamed down his muzzle from a gash over his left eye. His hind leg had been cut open on the rocks. Pain shot through his haunches and up his back. But he kept on swimming. As he approached the ship, he saw the ring buoy and the rope twisted around the rocks near the stern of the ship. The waves continued to pummel him, squeezing his ribs until he could hardly breathe. Each breath he took brought a sharp, knifing pain to his side. The slippery boulders loomed above him like icebergs.

When he reached the ring buoy, Skipper grasped the rope in his teeth and pulled. It held fast. Realizing the rope was caught underwater, the dog dove down. He clamped the rope in his jaws. He wrestled with it, but it did not budge. He came up for air, snorting and wheezing.

Everyone on the ship watched in awe and horror. The crew didn't have another rope to throw to the dog. All the others were too short or had been washed overboard. Even though the dog was fighting gallantly, they feared he would drown before their very eyes. Watching him was heartbreaking.

The wind increased. Hail pelted Skipper's head. The dog dove again. Taking the rope in his aching jaws, he braced his feet against the rocks that held it and strained with all his might. The rope loosened. Skipper snapped his head back and forth, as if playing tug-of-war with Colleen. The rope finally came free. Using the last of his breath, Skipper shoved off and swam up with the rope in his mouth.

When he broke through the water's surface, he heard the ocean's roar and the cheers from the ship.

But his job wasn't finished yet. Skipper swam around and faced the shore, readying for his final battle.

When Colleen saw the passengers shouting and waving, she jumped up and down. "He's alive! He's alive!" she yelled. "He's got the rope!" She held her forearm in front of her face in a futile attempt to block the snow. Another tremendous wave swelled behind Skipper as he headed toward shore. Colleen knew it would swallow the dog and hoped he could survive another pounding.

The wave crested. Its white foam boiled up and then cascaded down. Skipper paddled as hard as he could. But he couldn't outswim the wall of water. The fist of the wave hit him, enveloping him in total blackness.

*Skipper swam around and faced the shore,
readying for his final battle.*

The undertow coiled the rope around him, but he refused to loosen his bite on it. The dog fought on, even as his strength faltered.

He gradually began to lose feeling in his legs. The creeping numbness made them feel like wooden stumps. The seawater choked him, and his lungs burned.

Skipper summoned his last bit of strength and burst through the sea foam with the lifeline still gripped securely in his jaws. The dog's legs trembled as he staggered in the shallow waters, so close to shore. His blurry eyes searched for Colleen. He finally collapsed onto his side. His eyes closed, but the rope was still firmly clenched in his teeth.

Mr. Reilly and Mike Lawrence splashed through the swirling surf. Mike took the rope, and with his free hand he helped Mr. Reilly drag the dog onto the beach. Her heart racing, Colleen ran to Skipper. He wasn't moving and blood ran down his nose and hind leg. She buried her face in his cold, wet fur. *You can't die now!* she thought. *I can't bear to lose you.* Her mother handed her a blanket and she tenderly wrapped it around him. Enveloped in shock and fear, Colleen hugged him tighter.

Slowly she felt movement. Skipper shivered and his dark brown eyes opened. He was alive! Standing up on wobbly legs like a newborn colt, the Newfoundland shrugged off the blanket and began shaking the icy water off his coat.

CHAPTER TWELVE

RESCUE

Sheets of wind, water, and snow continued to batter the ship. The passengers and crew huddled on the deck, anxiously watching the dog's struggle. They were astounded that the dog had somehow managed to hang on to the rope, and when he reached shore, they were ecstatic. They cried and hugged each other.

Wrapped in a soggy blanket, Patrick squatted against the wall of the passageway and shivered, trying to get out of the wind. When he heard the cry of relief, he looked up.

"The dog made it!" Fergus screamed.

Patrick jumped up and hugged Fergus. "He did it!"

The ship's whistle had alerted people from Sally's Cove, and Patrick saw that a few other men and women had gathered on the beach to help.

He watched as the people on shore tied the rope to the tree on the cliff. But he knew their fight for survival wasn't over yet. Looking around at the soaked passengers, he saw that some were freezing and dazed, almost lifeless. They couldn't last much longer.

As soon as the rope was tightened enough to bear weight, Captain Flannery called to the crew. "Hook up that breeches buoy to the cable. We'll take everyone over, one at a time."

The captain double-checked the ring life buoy fitted with canvas breeches to make sure it was firmly attached to the cable.

"Fergus, go across first so you can help everyone as they reach the shore," ordered Captain Flannery.

"Aye, aye, sir," said Fergus as he saluted, then grabbed the rope and lowered himself into the breeches buoy. It swayed back and forth in the frosty gale.

The men on shore steadied the rope. They strained, clamping down harder as Fergus in the breeches buoy slowly began moving across the angry waves.

"'Tis a foolish man that angers the banshees—so I shall join them in their song," shouted Fergus. "This shellback won't be endin' up as flotsam! Eeeeeeeeeaaaahhhhhh!" he howled as he glided over the stormy water. The glacial wind churned the waves underneath him. To fall into them would mean certain death.

As Fergus reached the safety of land, Patrick waved his arms and yelled, "He made it!"

Mr. Reilly attached the breeches buoy to the other pulley line and sent it back to the ship. One by one, the women and children were ferried over the turbulent sea in the breeches buoy.

The groans, creaks, and splintering sounds from the listing ship grew louder. "We must hurry," the captain shouted hoarsely. "The *Ethie* is breaking up!"

It was Mrs. Daren and little Emily's turn. The mother wanted to carry her baby with her, but she would need to hold on to the buoy with both hands.

"We'll have to use a different method to get the wee one across," explained the captain. "We need something to put the baby in."

"I know what we can use," said Patrick. "I'll be right back." He lowered himself down through the ventilator shaft and crawled into the cargo hold of the ship. Dirty, icy bilgewater sloshed up his thighs. Alarmed at how fast the ship was filling, he seized a mail pouch and took it up on deck.

"Will this do, Captain?" asked Patrick.

"We'll make it work."

Her eyes wide in fear, the worried mother bundled her baby up in a shawl and carefully placed her in the leather mailbag. Emily began to cry as soon as she left the comfort of her mother's arms. Alice Daren's heart was breaking. She was scared to death, but she knew this was the only hope for her baby.

The captain lashed the mail pouch to the buoy and steadied it carefully. He waited for Mrs. Daren's final approval. Anxiety showed on her grim face as she nodded. Captain Flannery gave the mail pouch a gentle push.

As the mail pouch moved along the cable, it tossed in the blasts of wind. Enormous waves surged beneath the vulnerable cargo. About halfway across, a large wave crested, threatening to engulf the mailbag. Masses of white foam spewed up around the bag.

"She's falling!" Mrs. Daren screamed.

But the mailbag was not pulled from the line. When the pouch reached the shore, strong arms quickly hauled it in, and one of the men handed the bag to Colleen's father.

"Why in the world did they bother to send mail over?" he asked. Peering inside, he exclaimed, "Jesus, Mary, and Joseph! It's a baby!" Mr. Reilly gently handed the baby to Colleen.

Kicking her tiny hands and feet, the baby puckered up her face and started to cry again.

Colleen wrapped the squalling baby in a blanket and tried to comfort her. "There, there, wee one," she murmured. "The angels were watching over you. That's for certain." She kissed the baby's forehead. Skipper kept butting his head into Colleen's arm until she pulled the edge of the blanket down so he could sniff the baby. Satisfied, Skipper turned back to watch the rescue.

The mother of the baby came over next in the breeches buoy, relieved to be reunited with her daughter. Colleen placed the sobbing infant in her mother's arms. Mrs. Daren wrapped her body around Emily's, rocking back and forth. Eventually the baby began to calm down. Mrs. Reilly led Mrs. Daren and the other women and children up to the Reillys' small cottage for shelter.

One by one, the passengers evacuated the wrecked ship. "I can't swim," Reginald Warren whined, balking when his turn came. He appealed to the captain for support.

"Get up there, now!" ordered the captain. "Half the people on this ship can't swim. If you fall in the ocean,

One by one, the passengers were ferried over the turbulent sea in the breeches buoy.

knowing how to swim won't help anyway. You'll be pulverized on the rocks first."

As Mr. Warren protested, Patrick and a seaman hoisted him up, and off he went.

When Patrick and the crewmen were safely on the beach, it was the captain's turn. He was the last to leave the foundering vessel. Although grateful that all the passengers and crew had made it to safety, Captain Flannery grieved for his doomed ship.

"You are a good ship and I'll never forget you," he said, his eyes slowly sweeping the *Ethie* from her bow to her stern. "Thank you for delivering us safely through the storm." With that, the captain saluted the *Ethie,* tucked the ship's log into his coat, and swung himself into the breeches buoy. With no one left aboard to hold the ropes, he was worried that the separate line they had used to drag the breeches buoy back to the ship might get tangled with the main pulley line. Rather than taking a chance on getting stranded before he reached the shore, he leaned out and cut the other rope. He signaled the men on the beach, and they pulled him across by the pulley line. All ninety-two people on board had been saved.

On shore, Patrick watched with the others as the ship succumbed to her fate. Her timbers groaning, the *Ethie* shuddered under the relentless impact of the wind and waves. Wave after wave ripped into her, threatening to tear her apart piece by piece.

Patrick lifted his chin, letting the sleet hit his face. A deep sadness overwhelmed him and tears welled up in his eyes. He turned away. Then he felt something cold and wet touch his hand. It was a dog's muzzle.

"Skipper! Come here, boy!" Colleen called.

"Skipper it is, then," said Patrick, laughing. "Well, me boy. We're all alive because of you!" Patrick ruffled the fur on Skipper's head. "I'll not soon be forgetting that!"

Colleen smiled. None of them would ever forget this day. Patrick stared into the girl's eyes. He knew that the lives of the rescuers on shore and each person on the ship were forever linked to one another.

The survivors were dazed, wet, and chilled to the bone. They needed food, warmth, and shelter until the storm blew itself out. Mr. Reilly and Mike Lawrence offered their cottages. They could make room for several people if everyone slept on the floor side by side.

More people had arrived from Sally's Cove with sleighs to transport the rest of the survivors. The poor fishing families welcomed the half-frozen strangers into their homes, six or seven to a house. Each family willingly shared the food supplies they had stored for the winter with the grateful survivors.

⚓ ⚓ ⚓

The storm raged on for several days. The blizzard had blown down the telegraph wires, so it was impossible to send messages. For days, distraught relatives and the rest of Newfoundland believed that the *Ethie* had sunk. Throngs of people milled around outside the Reid offices in St. John's, hoping for information. When no word came, they assumed the worst. It was all too common a story. They had grown up hearing stories about the ships that often disappeared without a trace in Newfoundland's treacherous waters. Announcements appeared in newspapers that the SS *Ethie* was lost at sea and all aboard were feared dead. The entire nation mourned.

Only a few days before Christmas, the wicked storm subsided, and the telegraph wires on the island were patched together. A joyous message flashed across the wires and was received by the Minister of Justice of Bonne Bay:

The *Ethie* went ashore at Martin's Point, 18 miles north of Bonne Bay, at noon in Thursday's (December 11th) blizzard. Newfoundland dog swam with cable to help foundering ship. Sixty-two passengers and crew of thirty all safely landed by means of cable and breeches buoy. Steamer a total wreck.

(Sgd.) M. L. Powell

CHAPTER THIRTEEN

ST. JOHN'S, NEWFOUNDLAND

MAY 1921

Colleen stood on the platform with her mother, her father, and Skipper. Her hand rested on Skipper's head as he sat beside her, his tail thumping rhythmically against the floor. Straightening her shoulders, she lifted her chin and let the sun warm her face. A breeze blew her yellow hair ribbons across her face.

The Reillys had traveled to St. John's to attend a ceremony honoring Skipper's bravery. A photographer asked the family to pose with their dog so he could shoot their picture. Colleen wrinkled her nose as smoke puffs from the camera blew her way.

She looked around at the large crowd to see if she could spot any of the *Ethie*'s passengers and crew. A burst of raucous laughter caught her attention. There on the sidelines was Fergus, talking away while a group of reporters scribbled notes. She had heard that Fergus, having had enough of the cold Newfoundland gales, had moved back down to Ocracoke Island and his beloved Outer Banks. Colleen was pleased that he had traveled such a distance to be here.

Captain Flannery sat in the front row, his blue uniform neatly pressed and his brass buttons gleaming. He was now captain of another Reid ship, the SS *Kyle*.

There wasn't a more famous or respected sea captain in all of Newfoundland.

Standing next to the captain and his family was a deeply tanned Patrick Logan. With Fergus's assistance, he had been able to gain a berth as a sailor on a schooner that made trips down to the Outer Banks. He and Colleen often wrote to one another. She anxiously awaited his letters. They were full of exciting tales, although she suspected that some of them were just blarney.

A noisy flock of seagulls flew overhead. Colleen glanced up at them against the bright, blue sky and then looked back over the crowd of people gathered before her. The last time she had seen most of these people, they were bundled up in blankets and covered with snow. It was good to see them again, safe and happy and warm. She knew the wreck had changed all of them—crew, passengers, and rescuers—forever.

Her thoughts were interrupted when a man stood up and went to the podium.

"Good afternoon, ladies and gentlemen," he said. "My name is Reginald Warren. I am an executive with the Reid Company."

Colleen noticed how uncomfortable the man looked, shifting from one foot to the other.

"On behalf of my company and my fellow passengers on board the *Ethie*," he continued, "I would like to express our gratitude to Captain Flannery and his crew for their fine seamanship. I offer our deepest thanks to all the families of Martin's Point and Sally's Cove for their kind and generous hospitality, but most especially to the Reilly family and their dog Skipper."

Colleen looked down at Skipper. When he heard his name, the dog stood and wagged his tail. It looked almost as if he was grinning at the applauding crowd.

Mr. Warren then introduced Governor Charles Alexander Harris of Newfoundland, who stepped to the podium and called the Reilly family forward. After offering them his official thank-you, he bent over and placed around Skipper's neck a leather collar bearing a silver plate engraved with the word *Hero*. Wagging his tail, Skipper licked the governor's hand.

As the crowd applauded even louder, Skipper turned and stretched his head. Searching with his nose, the dog flared his nostrils. When he recognized the scent, his tail wagged. He trotted off the platform and padded into the applauding crowd.

"Doggie!" Little Emily squirmed away from her mother and dodged her father. Toddling over to Skipper, she grasped the big dog's fur in her tiny hands.

The governor shook hands with Colleen and her parents. As the officials congratulated Mr. and Mrs. Reilly, Colleen slipped away and joined Skipper with the Daren family. She was talking with Mrs. Daren when Patrick walked up and greeted them.

"I'd like to take a look at that collar," he said, smiling at Colleen. He bent down and gave Skipper a hug. "You are a fine dog," he said. "When I become the captain of my own ship, I'm going to have a dog just like you by my side."

"When you're captain of your own ship," said Colleen,

"come back to Sally's Cove. Maybe by then I'll be a veterinarian, and I can find just the right puppy for you."

At that moment several seagulls circled overhead, squawking loudly. Skipper lifted his head and woofed back, the silver plate on his new collar glinting in the sunlight.

Colleen smiled, thinking what a grand day it was.

৬৬৬ THE END ৬৬৬

In 1920, less than a year after the wreck of the Ethie, *Edwin J. Pratt, later named poet laureate of Canada, wrote this poem describing the dog that helped in the rescue.*

CARLO

I see no use in not confessing—
To trace your breed would keep me guessing;
It would indeed an expert puzzle
To match such legs with a jet-black muzzle.
To make a mongrel, as you know,
It takes some fifty types or so,
And nothing in your height or length,
In stand or colour, speed or strength,
Could make me see how any strain
Could come from mastiff, bull, or Dane.
But, were I given to speculating
On pedigrees in canine rating,
I'd wager this—not from your size,
Not merely from your human eyes,
But from the way you held that cable
Within those gleaming jaws of sable,

CARLO

Leaped from the taffrail of the wreck
With ninety souls upon its deck,
And with your cunning dog-stroke tore
Your path unerring to the shore—
Yes, stake my life, the way you swam,
That somewhere in your line a dam,
Shaped to this hour by God's own hand,
Had mated with a Newfoundland.

They tell me, Carlo, that your kind
Has neither conscience, soul, nor mind;
That reason is a thing unknown
To such as dogs; to man alone
The spark divine—he may aspire
To climb to heaven or even higher;
But God has tied around the dog
The symbol of his fate, the clog.
Thus, I have heard some preachers say—
Wise men and good, in a sort o' way—
Proclaiming from the sacred box
(Quoting from Butler and John Knox)
How freedom and the moral law
God gave to man, because He saw
A way to draw a line at root
Between the human and the brute,
And you were classed with things like bats,
Parrots and sand-flies and dock-rats,
Serpents and toads that dwell in mud,
And other creatures with cold blood
That sightless crawl in slime, and sink.
Gadsooks! It makes me sick to think

THE WRECK OF THE ETHIE

That man must so exalt his race
By giving dogs a servile place;
Prate of his transcendentalism,
While you save men by mechanism.
And when I told them how you fought
The demons of the storm, and brought
That life-line from the wreck to shore,
And saved those ninety souls or more,
They argued with such confidence—
'Twas instinct, nature, or blind sense.
A *man* could know when he would do it;
You did it and never knew it.

And so, old chap, by what they say,
You live and die and have your day,
Like any cat or mouse or weevil
That has no sense of good and evil
(Though sheep and goats, when they have died,
The Good Book says are classified);
But you, being neuter, go to—well,
Neither to heaven nor to hell.

I'll not believe it, Carlo; I
Will fetch you with me when I die,
And, standing up at Peter's wicket,
Will urge sound reasons for your ticket;
I'll show him your life-saving label
And tell him all about that cable,
The storm along the shore, the wreck,
The ninety souls upon the deck;
How one by one they came along,
The young and old, the weak and strong—

CARLO

Pale women, sick and tempest-tossed,
With children given up for lost;
I'd tell him more, if he would ask it—
How they tied a baby in a basket,
While a young sailor, picked and able,
Moved out to steady it on the cable;
And if he needed more recital
To admit a mongrel without title,
I'd get down low upon my knees,
And swear before the Holy Keys,
That judging by the way you swam,
Somewhere within your line, a dam
Formed for the job by God's own hand,
Had littered for a Newfoundland.

I feel quite sure that if I made him
Give ear to that, I could persuade him
To open up the Golden Gate
And let you in; but should he state
That from your legs and height and speed
He still had doubts about your breed,
And called my story of the cable
A cunningly devised fable,
Like other rumours that you've seen
In Second Peter, one, sixteen,
I'd tell him (saving his high station)
The devil take his legislation,
And, where life, love, and death atone,
I'd move your case up to the Throne.

November 1920
Edwin J. Pratt

105

AUTHOR'S NOTE

Is this a true story?

Yes. This book is based on the true story of the shipwreck that occurred on the remote western coast of Newfoundland on December 11, 1919. That day, the coastal steamer SS *Ethie* was caught in one of the worst blizzards in Newfoundland's history, and the winds and waves hurled her onto the rocks just offshore at Martin's Point. All of the crew and passengers were saved from the wrecked ship. The first newspaper accounts describing the wreck and the rescue told of the Newfoundland dog's heroism.

To help with the sense of the story, I fictionalized some elements. I added some characters and, to preserve the privacy of family members of the actual persons involved, I also changed the names of the characters. The dog's real name was Wisher.

The SS Ethie, *a coastal steamer built in 1900, carried passengers and cargo around the coast of Newfoundland.*

The SS Ethie *at her mooring in a quiet bay. Her pump is cleaning out the bilgewater. Note the Black Labrador Retriever sitting on the beach and the Newfoundland dog in the water.*

Some later accounts have disputed aspects of the story, but I believe that, based on the primary and secondary sources I consulted, the core of the events I have described in this book are accurate.

How much do we know about the wreck of the Ethie?

The first newspaper accounts, released by the Associated Press and dated December 17, 24, and 31, 1919, tell us that the SS *Ethie* piled up on the rocks off Martin's Point during a major storm. The articles describe how fishermen on shore rigged up a life-saving device and hauled the ninety-two passengers and crew to safety. The reports noted that news of the rescue did not reach the outside world right away because all the telegraph lines were downed by the storm.

The articles and reports tell us that Walter Young, the purser on the *Ethie*, happened to be familiar with the area and helped navigate the ship to the cove off

Martin's Point. Chief Engineer Paddy Burton and his crew battled to keep the engines' steam pressure up so the ship could stay away from the dangerous north-western Newfoundland coast during that long night of December 10. First Officer John Gullage gave the captain helpful advice.

Captain Edward English, at thirty-seven years of age, showed remarkable leadership under such dire conditions. Written accounts confirm that Captain English was later awarded a silver tankard for his role in the rescue and for his outstanding seamanship. A plate on the tankard reads "Presented to Captain English by the government of Newfoundland in recognition of his gallant conduct and able seamanship which resulted in the saving of all the passengers and crew numbering 92 souls on the occasion of the wreck of the SS *Ethie* near Cow Head in December, 1919."

I consulted several documents as primary sources of information. Foremost is the ship's log, which details dates, times, and weather information from the *Ethie*'s last voyage. The log, the crew manifest, and photographs of the SS *Ethie* are owned by the Maritime History Archives of Memorial University of Newfoundland, located in St. John's.

I found many helpful secondary sources at the Provincial Research Library Division in the Arts and Culture Centre, located in St. John's, Newfoundland, which contains books as well as magazine and newspaper articles outlining the dramatic rescue. The reports tell us that when the people onboard tried to get a line

The SS Ethie *shortly after she ran aground at Martin's Point on December 11, 1919.*

from the ship to the shore, it became entangled in the rocks surrounding the *Ethie*. Fishermen on the beach realized that they could not reach the steamer by boat, so they sent a Newfoundland dog through the treacherous waters to fetch the rope. Also, J. R. Smallwood's *Stories of Newfoundland*, the Source Book for Teachers published by the Canadian Department of Education, includes a section called "The Loss of the *Ethie*." This story describes the rescue by the Newfoundland dog as well as the saving of the baby in the ship's mailbag.

How much do we know about the dog who helped with the rescue?

Tom Decker of Parson's Pond, Newfoundland, told me that in 1919 his father, Reuben Decker, a fisherman, lived alone on Martin's Point with his dog, Wisher.

Accounts vary about the breed of the dog. The day of the shipwreck, December 11, was Reuben Decker's twenty-sixth birthday. Tom Decker's father had not told him many details of the rescue, but Reuben Decker did say that many months after the rescue he had traveled to St. John's, where the governor of Newfoundland, Charles Alexander Harris, presented Wisher with a leather collar bearing a silver plate inscribed with the word *Hero*. The collar given to Wisher, unfortunately, has been lost.

Was a baby really saved in a mailbag?
Yes. The baby's mother, Mrs. Elizabeth Batten, kept the mail pouch from the *Ethie*. In 1986, Hilda Batten

Hilda Batten Menchions—the baby who was rescued from the shipwreck—donated to the Gros Morne National Park the mailbag from the Ethie *that was used in the rescue.*

The small museum at the Lobster Cove Head lighthouse displays artifacts from the SS Ethie.

Menchions, the last living survivor of the shipwreck—the baby in the mailbag—donated the mailbag to the Gros Morne National Park in western Newfoundland. Mrs. Menchions told me that her mother, who was pregnant with a second baby at the time of the shipwreck, rarely spoke of the terrifying experience but kept the precious mailbag that had saved her young daughter.

Can we see the remains of the ship and artifacts from the rescue?

Yes. The small museum at the Lobster Cove Head Lighthouse near Bonne Bay, just north of Rocky Harbour, displays the mailbag from the *Ethie*.

In the Gros Morne National Park, a historical marker on Highway 430 shows the location of the shipwreck. In the rocky, windswept cove at Martin's Point, around three miles north of Sally's Cove, we can still see the rusted remains of the SS *Ethie*. As visitors view her final resting place, it is easy for them to imagine the terror and hopelessness that the crew and the passengers

In the rocky, windswept cove at Martin's Point, Newfoundland, visitors today can still see the rusted remains of parts from the SS Ethie.

on the *Ethie* must have felt and their enormous relief and gratitude when they were so miraculously rescued.

What is the importance of the poem "Carlo"?

I included the poem "Carlo," on page 102, because I believe it was written about the *Ethie*. Edwin J. Pratt, who was later named poet laureate of Canada, wrote the poem in 1920, just months after the wreck. The poem does not mention the ship by name or the location of the shipwreck, but details make it clear that Pratt is writing about the wreck of the *Ethie*. The dog, named Carlo in the poem, is at least part Newfoundland and swims with the lifeline to the shore during a storm, saving more than ninety souls. The people on the ship save the baby by placing it in a "basket" and sending it to shore.

Published by
THE STAR
PUBLISHING CO., LTD.
A. L. Barrett,
Manager

★ THE WESTERN STAR ★

"THE ONLY
NEWSPAPER ON
THE WEST
COAST"

PRICE: $1.00 PER YEAR • WEDNESDAY, DECEMBER 17, 1919 • FOREIGN: $2.00 PER YEAR

The Reid Nfld. Co.'s SS Ethie, built in 1900 at Glasgow, Scotland, by A. and J. Inglis shipbuilders, was 154.7 feet in length with a steel hull and a draft of 12.6 feet.

GIRL WINS FATHER LIBERTY

etter to Judge Causes
Parent from Jail

S. S. "ETHIE" VICTIM OF STORM

ASHORE AT MARTIN POINT

Curling, N. F., Dec. 16—The s. s. Ethie went ashore at Martin Point, between Cow Head and Bonne Bay, during last week's storm and became a total wreck. Capt. English, his crew and passengers escaped and reached Bonne Bay. The Ethie was engaged in the coastal trade between Bay of Islands and Labrador, and is the second of the Reid Nfld. Co.'s fleet of steamers to end her days on the North West Coast. She was on the way south, having left Cow Head at 8 o'clock Wednesday evening for Bonne Bay, hoping to reach that port before the bursting of the impending storm. But the storm came on shortly after the ship put out. Particulars of her going ashore are not yet to hand.

The telegraph line to Bonne Bay was put out of commission by the gale, and it was impossible to hear from that section of the country. When the ship, however, did not turn up by the end of the week, much concern was felt for her safety, and the various wireless stations were applied to for any tidings of her. But nothing

could be learned of her fate until Monday evening, when a messenger reached Deer Lake from Bonne Bay with the intelligence as cited above.

LATER

The Ethie, unable to stem the raging hurricane, drifted from daylight on Thursday till noon, when she was beached. A line was fired from the ship, but got caught up amongst the boulders, so the people of Martin Point sent out one of their dogs, a very sagacious animal, to bring it ashore. The ship had sixty passengers on board, and her crew numbered thirty-two; all of whom were safely landed by means of a boatswain's chair on a line set up from the ship to the shore. One little baby of eighteen months of age was transferred to land in a mail bag. All underwent a most thrilling experience, and suffered much from intense cold. No doubt when full particulars are learnt it will be found that their miraculous escape from the deep was due in no small measure to the skilful seamanship of Captain English.

BENEVOLENT
D TO CHEER
ROOPS

been done. This year relatively little is heard of the soldiers and sailors. This year relatively little is heard of the soldiers and sailors; nonetheless, there are countless wounded and shell-shocked young men in base hospitals

GLOSSARY OF NAUTICAL TERMS

AFT—in, at, or toward the rear of a boat

ASTERN—see **STERN**

AVAST—a nautical command to stop

BAROMETER—a weather tool used to measure air pressure

BO'SUN OR **BOATSWAIN**—a ship's officer in charge of riggings, sails, anchors, cables, etc. and all work on deck; the bo'sun details the crew to carry out the day to day work of the ship

BOW (bäu)—the front of a boat

BOWLINE (bäu-line)—the line used to tow or secure a boat; or (bo-lin) a kind of knot

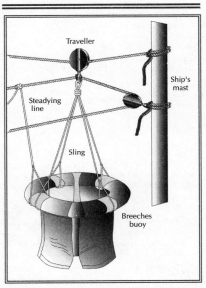

Traveller

Ship's mast

Steadying line

Sling

Breeches buoy

BREECHES (britchez) **BUOY**—a canvas seat hung from a life buoy used to haul persons from ship to shore, especially during rescue operations

BULKHEAD—a partition between compartments on a ship

BULWARK—the side of a ship above the upper deck

BUOY (boo-ee)—a floating object, usually used for rescue or to mark something lying underwater

CHRONOMETER—a precise clock, often used in navigation

DAVIT—a crane used to raise or lower boats or cargo over the side of a ship

DORY—a small flat-bottomed wooden boat with high, sloping sides and a sharp bow

FLOTSAM—floating wreckage, cargo, or debris

ABOUT THE AUTHOR

www. hilary hyland. com

Hilary Hyland is a former hotel
industry executive. Hyland lives
with her husband and daughter
and two dogs in Centreville,
Virginia, where she writes full time
and gives author presentations and
speaking engagements.

Hilary Hyland would love to
hear from her readers. You may
email her at hilaryhyland@aol.com.

GLOSSARY

FORE—in, at, or toward the front of a boat

FORECASTLE (foc-sl)—the forward part of the upper deck of a ship; the crew's quarters, usually in a ship's bow

GUNWALE (gun-l)—the upper edge of the side of a boat

HARDTACK—a saltless hard biscuit

HOLD—the interior of a ship below decks where cargo is stored

HULL—the outer structure of a boat or ship

JETTISON—to throw cargo overboard, often to lighten a ship's load especially in time of distress

LEE—the side of a boat or ship sheltered from the wind

LIMEY—nickname for a British sailor

PITCHPOLE—to flip end over end

PORT—the left side of a boat or ship

RUDDER—a vertical blade, extending from the stern into the water, that pivots to turn a boat or ship

RIGGING—the lines and cables on a ship supporting the mast

SCUPPER—an opening in the bulwarks of a ship that allows water falling on deck to flow overboard

SHELLBACK—an old or veteran sailor

SKIFF—a small boat

SOUTHWESTER OR **SOU'WESTER**—a storm with fierce winds and rain from the southwest; an oilskin storm hat with a long brim on the sides and back to keep rain off the wearer's neck

STARBOARD—the right side of a boat or ship

STEM—the main upright at the bow of a ship

STERN—the rear of a boat or ship

TAFFRAIL—a rail around the stern of a ship

WINDLASS—a winch, often shaped like a barrel that a line or chain wraps around, used to hoist or haul objects such as the anchor.